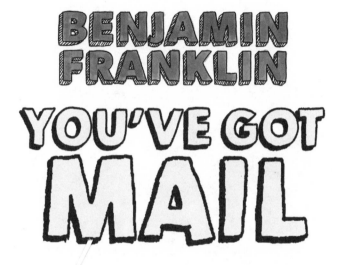

BENJAMIN FRANKLIN
YOU'VE GOT MAIL

BENJAMIN FRANKLIN YOU'VE GOT MAIL

New York Times #1 Best-Selling Author
by **ADAM MANSBACH**

Thurber Award–Winning Author
and **ALAN ZWEIBEL**

Dɪsɴᴇʏ • HYPERION

Los Angeles   New York

Also by Adam Mansbach & Alan Zweibel
Benjamin Franklin: Huge Pain in My . . .

First Edition, May 2017
1 3 5 7 9 10 8 6 4 2
FAC-020093-17076
Printed in the United States of America

This book is set in Adobe Caslon Pro, American Writer, Cute Letters Heartless, John Doe, Progeny/Fontspring; Futura LT Pro, Century 725/Monotype; Grilled Cheese BTN/Fontbros
Designed by Tyler Nevins

Library of Congress Cataloging-in-Publication Data

Names: Mansbach, Adam, 1976- author. | Zweibel, Alan, author.
Title: Benjamin Franklin : you've got mail / Adam Mansbach & Alan Zweibel.
Description: First edition. | Los Angeles; New York : Disney-Hyperion, [2017] | Series: Benjamin Franklin ; book 2 | Summary: "Ike Saturday travels back to 1776 to help Benjamin Franklin keep history on track"—Provided by publisher.
Identifiers: LCCN 2016040469 (print) | LCCN 2017000208 (ebook) | ISBN 9781484713051 (hardback) | ISBN 1484713052 (hardcover) | ISBN 9781484714478 | ISBN 1484714474
Subjects: | CYAC: Time travel—Fiction. | Franklin, Benjamin, 1706-1790—Fiction. | Letters—Fiction. | Dating (Social customs)—Fiction. | Stepfamilies—Fiction. | United States—History—Revolution, 1775-1783—Fiction. | France—History—Louis XVI, 1774-1793—Fiction. | BISAC: JUVENILE FICTION / Historical / United States / Colonial & Revolutionary Periods. | JUVENILE FICTION / School & Education. | JUVENILE FICTION / Humorous Stories.
Classification: LCC PZ7.1.M367 Bh 2017 (print) | LCC PZ7.1.M367 (ebook) | DDC [Fic]—dc23
LC record available at https://lccn.loc.gov/2016040469

Reinforced binding
Visit www.DisneyBooks.com

For Zachary, Lexi, Jordan, Kylie, and Sydney —AZ
For Max and Jed —AM

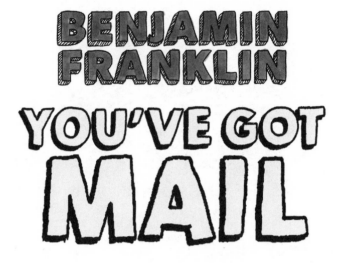

CHAPTER 1

Traveling backward through two hundred and thirty-nine years of Time in a cardboard box is less comfortable than you might think, if you are bad at thinking. But comfort was not on my mind, because I was too busy being terrified that Claire Wanzandae and I had ruined the future of the Republic by sending a map and a peanut butter and jelly sandwich back to 1776, and hoping that my close personal amigo Benjamin Franklin—Founding Father, statesman, inventor, printer, author, politician, scientist, musician, philosopher, and creator of the Very postal system I was now Abusing—had not been stomped to death by a bunch of colonial Butt Monkeys.

In case this Tale is being read by intelligent machines or disgusting space aliens from the distant future, or even by regular people who do not know how I got myself in this Predicament, let me remind you. A few weeks ago, although it seems like years, I wrote a letter, put an Old Timey Colonial Stamp on it, and sent it to Benjamin Franklin. I stole this stamp from the collection of my stepfather, Dirk the Jerk, but that is not important. What is important is that the letter arrived in BF's mailbox in the year 1776. And once we both stopped not believing who the other person Was, BF and I became pen pals. It turned out we had a lot in common, because my junior high school is a vipers' nest of backbiting and clique-building and fart jokes, and Colonial politics is exactly the same.

Anyway, me and Claire—who at the time was just a tall, funny girl with hair that smelled like cherry blossoms and gasoline, but is now my actual girlfriend—started trying to help Benjamin Franklin with the war against the British, which was just about to get Cracking back in 1776. So we sent a map of the country, which my history teacher said they could have desperately used for military planning, and also a peanut butter and jelly sandwich, which we renamed a Claireike and figured we could invent before the British, robbing the enemy of its greatest Thing and also securing our own place in history. But unfortunately the jelly stuck the map to the back of the Declaration of Independence thanks to some very sloppy handling on the part of one of the Founding Fathers, so when they sent the Declapendence to the newspaper to share with the world, the printer included the map. This made BF and the other Founding Fathers look insane, what with all the made-up states, and also caused King George of Britain to realize it wasn't just thirteen insignificant Colonies he was losing, but a whole Vast continent. His next move was probably going to be sending fourteen Bazillion troops over there, which meant good-bye Independence, hello Staying a British Colony Forever.

The last time I heard from B-Freezy, he had just been dropped off on the steps of the Philadelphia post office by a horse 'n' buggy thief called the Young Scamp, and things were not looking so good, in the sense that his house had been burned down by an angry mob and now his Person was in danger of suffering a similar Fate. That was why I decided to tape myself up inside a giant box: I needed to save my friend, though I was Unsure how I would be received. On one hand, BF had made it abundantly clear that he did not want me to visit, by writing things such as "Do not under any circumstances visit." On the other hand, the last words of the last letter he had sent me were "HELP

HELP HELP," so my instincts were to try to get back to 1776 so I could HELP HELP HELP him.

Meanwhile, the other question that had me Vexed was: Would mailing myself back in time work, or would I end up Atomized to death for trying to mess with Physics? In theory, if paper and maps and peanut butter and jelly Claireikes could travel through time, then a Person shouldn't be any different. But there is Theory, and then there is Having No Idea And Possible Death. In which case the country and Ben Franklin were not going to get Saved, since I was pretty much the only chance either of them had, what with my remarkable Knowledge from the future.

Although another concern was: *What* remarkable knowledge from the future? I mean, I am in Honors History, but I'm only a B student. I know a lot about a few random things—such as Medicine Shows, which I did a research paper on, although that research paper was mainly based on a TV show I saw on the Discovery Channel. I'm pretty smart about the early days of baseball, but that is unlikely to help since the early days of baseball were about a hundred years later.

When it comes to Colonial History, there are probably dogs who know more.

You've Got Mail

I don't know how long I spent thinking these thoughts of Fear and Anxiousness, but at some point I must have drifted off to sleep. The box had airholes, but not enough of them, and the air in there was hot and close and stale, and I could feel my eyelids falling to half-mast and then quarter-mast and I remember thinking that it might be smart to sleep through as much of this journey as I could, because that beat worrying.

A giant rattling THUMP woke me, and for a second I forgot where I was and what I was doing, and I freaked out.

Then I remembered, and immediately freaked out again.

The first question was whether the THUMP was a thump of delivery or just a thump of being thrown onto a truck or into a sorting room or whatever. I lined up my eye with the box's biggest airhole, and when I peered through it I saw blue. Unless the ceiling of the truck or storage room was painted to look like the sky, that meant I was outside, and that was good enough for me. I grabbed the handy steak knife Claire Wanzandae had packed for me, along with a bottle of apple juice and a bologna and cheese Claireike, and cut a giant slit all the way across the top and stepped out into the world beyond the box.

The very first thing I saw was: a horse pooping right in

5

the middle of the street. He didn't even stop walking, just clop-clopped on his merry way, pulling some guy's carriage, the big narrow spindly wheels running right over the giant mound of waste a second later like it was no big deal.

Being highly Observant, I quickly deduced that I had done it. It had worked. This was 1776. For a moment, I allowed myself to feel a sense of relief and excitement, at 1) not being dead and 2) being probably the first time traveler in the history of the world. Then I took a longer look around, and the fact that my problems were Just beginning sat down on top of those feelings and crushed them to death.

To start with, there was the fact that there was, indeed, nothing left of Ben Franklin's house but a singed and smoldering wood frame, and some random deposits of semi-burned clothing and books and other assorted Belongings.

And a mailbox, which I had been Delivered to. Maybe as some kind of joke.

There were a dozen people on BF's block, mostly men but also a few women and one or two kids. Nobody seemed to have noticed that a giant mauled cardboard box had given birth to a Kid of the Future. For that matter, none of them seemed to be paying much attention to the hideous remains of BF's giant house, either. Which made me think that maybe his house burning down was Old News, and it had taken a couple of days for me to make my Epic Journey.

Which meant that Ben could be anywhere by now. Including dead, or New Jersey. Though hopefully Fate hadn't been so cruel.

 **CHAPTER 2**

My little sister, Carolyn, is really into these puzzle books where they show you two almost-identical pictures side by side, and you have to Notice ten things that are different between them—like, the girl's coat has three buttons on the left and four on the right, or there's a giant booger on the guy's face in one picture but not the other, though I'm just kidding about that last one. But that's what standing on Chestnut Street was like in those first few moments: the picture in my mind was from 2015, and the one in front of me was 1776, and in order to get my Bearings, I had to figure out what had changed.

Some of the differences were obvious, like Cars = Horse-Drawn Buggies, but a lot of them took more time to figure out, such as: Nobody is holding a takeout coffee cup. Nobody is walking a dog. There's the noise of talking, but underneath it is a kind of deeper quiet, because a million power lines and air conditioners and cable boxes aren't humming away at a subsonic level.

The biggest thing, though, was the fashion. That, I quickly Ascertained, was a problem that had to be confronted with Speed. Because if I was going to blend in here instead of getting pegged as some kind of freak and thrown into the loony bin, I was going to have to Obtain myself some gear. Thirty seconds of studying the people on the street told me that, and a lot more.

For instance, I had no idea how the women even walked, because most of them looked like they were wearing about eight skirts at once, plus some kind of squeezy corset thing up top, and then these weird broad-rimmed hats to finish it all off, so basically they looked like upside-down wineglasses tottering around.

The dudes, meanwhile, wore those penguin-type jackets, long in back and short in front and goofy all over. Plus these pants that I think are called breeches, which I assume is short for "breach of good taste." They ended at the knee, and got tucked into long socks of some kind. And craziest of all, practically every man was sporting a white wig, like it was You Can Imagine How Bad My Real Hair Looks If I'm Covering It With This Ridiculous White Wig Day or something. And then over the wigs, they wore those big triangular hats that I'd seen in pictures but in person looked like they were wearing huge throw pillows on their heads.

I, meanwhile, was wearing jeans and a polo shirt, and underneath that an ugly T-shirt Dirk the Jerk had given me last year when he went on a business trip, meaning he'd bought it at the Newark airport on his way back home. And a pair of Chuck Taylors.

I jogged onto BF's lawn and started poking around in the rubble for something to wear. I found a lightly burned coat that came down to my shins, took off my polo shirt, shrugged it on over my T-shirt, and buttoned it all the way to the neck. Then I pulled my socks up over my jeans and strode off Purposefully. I wasn't going to be any use to Ben or to America until I found myself a Haberdashery or whatever.

I made my way up the block with my heart hammering against my chest, half expecting all the people and even the horses to stop short at the sight of me and start pointing and whispering. But that type of thing never actually happens in real life, not even in Colonial times. We just think that way because each and every one of us secretly believes we're the center of the universe, with nobody, including Yours Truly, actually bothering to remember that the Other Guy is just as caught up in his own life and Feelings as you are in yours, and so we just barrel around acting like toolboxes all the time. If I could condense that Wisdom into about six words, I could give BF a run for his money, but I Cannot.

For a city on the brink of war, a city that had just burned down the home of its leading citizen, Philadelphia seemed pretty calm. People looked like they were going about their business, whatever that was. It was hard to imagine the angry mobs Ben had written about, which gave me Hope that I would find him alive and well. Especially if I got down to the business of Looking as soon as possible. And so I turned my attention to finding a Shoppe at which to purchase suitably idiotic Wearables.

After a short Jaunt and a lot of sweating beneath my heavy, too-big coat, I found myself standing across the street from a store whose sign read ALLERTON & SON FINE GARMENTS FOR MEN & BOYS, which might sound like a mouthful but was actually borderline catchy as names went in BF's neighborhood, for example in comparison to H.M. CROWDER'S PUB AND EATERY FEATURING FRESH DELECTABLES AND CHILLED OR HOT BEVERAGES FOR THE DISCERNING LADY AND GENTLEMAN, which was next door.

I took a deep breath, and walked inside.

CHAPTER 3

I don't do a whole lot of clothes shopping normally, because I hate going anywhere with my mom, especially if it involves her sitting outside a dressing room while I try on pants and she calls out stuff like "Is it too snug in the crotch, honey?" If anybody from school happened to walk into the store and see that, I'd have to fake my own death and cremation. But at the same time, dudes my age don't really shop together either, because that is also awkward. So usually, I just wait until Christmas or my birthday rolls around, and hope for the best.

That said, I had Sufficient experience to realize in approximately one millisecond that Allerton & Son was nothing like the Gap. There were no piles of clothes on display on racks or tables, just a counter with an old dude standing behind it in wire-rimmed spectacles and huge white puffy muttonchops that ate up half his face. Behind the counter, it looked like, was a stockroom.

"Good morning, young master," he greeted me. I figured he was Allerton, because if he was Son, Allerton would've been a hundred and twenty. "What might I do for you?"

"I'm in need of some Fine Garments," I said, and when he just smiled and blinked at me, I figured maybe I was being rude by not addressing him with a Form of Address like he had me, so I added, "Old Master."

Judging by the fart-sniffing way his face crinkled up, this was definitely the wrong choice. Or else he had just taken Note of my current Garments.

He recovered quickly though, probably because the customer is Always right (if that had been Declared yet, anyway, which it might have been by You Know Who), and said, "I daresay you are, my young friend."

He peered down over the counter, smiled, and said, "What, if I may inquire, are those contraptions currently afflicting your lower extremities? In all my years of haberdashery, I confess I've never seen their like."

I looked down at my Chucks, too, as if I was as surprised as he was, and said the first thing that popped into my head.

"They're from France. Everybody's wearing them over there."

Old Man Allerton chuckled. "I fear you have been deceived by some unscrupulous merchant, young master. But never fear: we shall outfit you with all due celerity. Remove your outer garment, if you please. Or, at any rate, whomever's outer garment it is that you currently comport yourself within."

I just stood there for a second, trying to translate the words into English. Luckily, Old Man Allerton didn't notice. He was already bustling around in the storeroom.

I figured it out, and slipped out of BF's coat just as he was turning back toward me, a couple pairs of pants and some kind of shirty-looking thing laid across his arms.

"Now then, my—" Old Man Allerton said, and then he looked up and gasped, eyes going dinner-plate wide behind the glasses.

"By all that is good and wholesome!" he practically shouted, dropping the clothes atop the counter. "What blasphemous and uncouth garment is this that now affronts my visage?"

His whole face was crimson, and he looked like he might keel over.

"Oh," I said. "Yeah, I guess it's kind of ugly. I can—"

He drew himself up taller, and interrupted. "Young master, I demand a swift explanation of the provocation against Our Lord painted so garishly across your tunic!"

I looked down, and suddenly understood the Magnitude of my own stupidity.

"Oh," I said. "It's okay. The New Jersey Devils are just, like, a sports team. It's got nothing to do with, you know, religion or Lucifer or Beelzebub or the Prince of Darkness or, well, you get my drift, right?"

His color deepened a shade, from crimson to dark scarlet. "What kind of sporting club would assign itself such an obscenity?"

I thought it was a rhetorical question, but after a couple seconds of his eyebrows bearing down on me, I realized Old Man Allerton was actually waiting for an answer.

"It was just a stupid joke," I mumbled. "We changed it."

"For the sake of your eternal soul, I should hope so!" He shook his head at me. "I pray no members of the fairer sex chanced to glimpse your attire as you traversed the thoroughfare!"

"No, sir," I said, trying to look all beaten down and remorseful. He couldn't yell at me forever, I figured.

15

Once again: wrong. "This merely confirms all I've long said of New Jersey—that foul, licentious swampland!"

"Look," I said, and peeled off the T-shirt, which was sweaty and disgusting anyway. "Here you go. You can throw it away for all I care, all right?"

"With enthusiasm," he said slowly, the color receding from his cheeks. "And I am glad to see that you have wits enough to realize the folly of your ways."

"Uh-huh," I said, and grabbed the stack of clothes he'd brought out.

Old Man Allerton was good with sizes. Everything fit me perfectly. Two minutes later, a vested, breeched, stockinged Franklin Isaac Saturday stared back from the mirror, from beneath a tricornered hat. Old Man Allerton looked incredibly satisfied with himself.

"That will be eight and one-half dollars, young master," Allerton sang out, his life back to normal now.

And like a Grade A moron, I reached into my pocket and handed Old Man Allerton a nice crispy twenty-dollar bill featuring a portrait of a man who was currently nine years old.

"What in tarnation is this?"

"Whoops," I said, snatching it back before he could look

Closer. "Sorry. Let me just, um, locate my billfold." I picked up BF's coat and started rifling through the pockets, hoping he'd have some doubloons or whatever stashed in there someplace, though I hadn't Noticed any before.

Old Man Allerton was watching me closely, and frowning up a storm.

"That garment is familiar to me," he said slowly. "I daresay I sold it to Mr. Benjamin Franklin, not two months ago." He reached forward, over the counter, fingered the bottom hem of the coat, and nodded. "This is my stitching, and the ambassador's coat."

And bam, he snatched it out of my hands.

"If you are one of the scoundrels who destroyed the ambassador's house, admit it now!" he roared. "And face my wrath, you foul villain!"

"No!" I said, backing away from the counter. "The ambassador is my friend! I borrowed it from him."

His eyes bored into me. "He is short on friends these days. How do I know you did not abscond with that great, persecuted man's garment?"

I shoved my hand into my back pocket. "See for yourself. Here's a letter he sent me. I'm telling you, he's like a grandfather to me."

Allerton snatched it out of my hand and brought it about an inch from his eyeball. After a moment, he lowered it and looked at me again.

"So it seems," he muttered, still looking at me skeptically.

"You don't know where I can find him, do you?" I asked.

Allerton pulled himself up to his full height. "He has not been seen since the unfortunate events of the night before last. Some say he has fled the city. Others, that he is in hiding, and others still that he met an unsavory and yet-undiscovered end—though I for one do not believe that a man of his wiles could possibly have succumbed to such a dismal fate."

"Me neither," I said. "As a matter of fact, I came to Philadelphia to find him."

"But you are just a boy! How can you poss—"

"Don't underestimate me," I said, and the way I said it was so fierce that Old Man Allerton didn't just shut up, he also started looking at me in a whole different way. Like, with respect. I decided to push my advantage while I could.

"Put my Fine Garments on Ben's account," I instructed him, and before Old Man Allerton could respond, I turned and marched out of the store, walking so straight it was like I had a steel rod for a spine. I felt bold and full of confidence, just from Declaring my intentions and beliefs. And while I had no idea Whatsoever of how to actually go about finding Ben—the first step in my journey to saving the future American population from playing soccer instead of football but still calling it football—I did have two things going for me now that I hadn't before. One was that I now looked like a proper Colonial bozo. The other was that I had an idea—an idea that I should have thought of the second I stepped out of my box, but hey, better late than Never.

The idea was: *Look in BF's mailbox, stupid.* Because if he had written to me, Claire Wanzandae would have forwarded the letter there.

I took off my sweaty tricornered hat, pulled up my dumb itchy stockings and my idiotic woolen breeches, sprinted back toward the rubble of Ben Franklin's house, and opened the mailbox.

Inside was a letter. And inside the letter was another letter.

I read the outside letter first.

CHAPTER 4

Dear Ike,

First of all, I am assuming that you are fine and traveled safely and are not a small pile of ash or anything unimaginably horrible like that. I am also assuming that you will write to me as soon as you possibly can to confirm this, because I am pretty concerned and definitely did not study enough for the history midterm today. I probably only got a B+, which as you know would be one of my lowest grades ever, because I'm a huge nerd. Also, and I shouldn't even tell you this because I'm sure you have more than enough problems to deal with, and as soon as you read the letter from BF inside this letter you might have even more—but your parents are extremely freaked out.

Sorry, I know Dirk the Jerk is not your parent, so I take back my usage of the plural. Your mom is extremely freaked out. I know this because she called me. I do not know how she got my number, but when I saw your number come up on my phone, my heart flew up into the sky like a helium balloon. Then when I heard your mom's voice instead of yours, the balloon hit a tree branch and popped.

Anyway, the note you left her to explain that you had not been kidnapped but were merely taking a short vacation from your life to Figure Things Out and would be back soon, and that she shouldn't worry or call the police . . . well, the good news is that she believes it. The bad news is that she is still scared out of her mind, though as far as I know she has not involved law enforcement. She seems to think that either your friend Ryan Demphill or I must know your whereabouts, so she keeps calling us both. But obviously Ryan doesn't know anything, and even more obviously I would never, ever betray your trust, so mostly I have just been trying to reassure her that you are safe and sound and will be back soon. I feel bad lying to her, but I guess it's one of those lies that's okay to tell because it protects a person from a truth that would really bother them.

Meanwhile, as you will see from the other letter, someone

who is not safe and sound is: Benjamin Franklin. But I know you will save him, Ike. I have one hundred percent confidence in you and I swear I will shut up in a second so you can read his letter and bust into action, but first I wanted to say that so far, the future (meaning the present) has not changed as far as I can tell. Like, I didn't wake up today to a breakfast of Bangers and Mash or Toad in the Gutter or whatever gross stuff British people eat. I'm not having a spot o' tea as I write this. I'm still Claire Wanzandae, and America is still America. Which means that there is still time, and hope. Whatever we have screwed up in the past has not yet rippled forward. It can still be fixed. That is my theory, anyway.

Okay, go now and read Ben's letter and go help him.

XO,
Claire

P.S. And write back.

P.P.S. But read Ben's letter first.

P.P.P.S. Hurry!

CHAPTER 5

Dear Ike and Claire Wanzandae—

As I sit cross-legged atop a bookcase in this Philadelphia branch of the US Post Office where I slept last night while hiding from the enraged mob whose collective wish was to detach my limbs from their rightful locations in the torso, my mind, as if in possession of a mind of its own, wanders to a Time when I invented the postal system. My vision was a series of small structures strategically deployed about the thirteen colonies that would act as a repository for parcels that would be dispatched to the recipient—and neither snow, nor rain, nor heat, nor gloom of night would stay those couriers from the swift completion of their appointed rounds.

At no moment in any planning phase did I consider the inclusion of a bed, a warm blanket, a bathtub, or a medicine cabinet with a surfeit of toiletries as necessary components in the postal experience. However, now that I have been sleeping atop a wooden counter while resting my head on a small scale and then, upon awakening with the sun, brushing my teeth with glue and flossing with cord, I do wish I had allowed for such hygienic provisions. Uncharacteristically nearsighted of me, and rather ironic given that I am also the inventor of bifocals, whose lower half correct the myopia I have figuratively exhibited.

I am growing hungry, Ike and Claire Wanzandae, and at this juncture it would be of little surprise to me if my stomach's rumblings could transcend the Atlantic and awaken King George III, his wife Charlotte of Mecklenburg-Strelitz, and their three children. For all I have had to consume since seeking refuge in this Postal Office two days ago is a crateful of peaches that a blacksmith from Georgia attempted to send to his mother here in Philadelphia for her sixty-eighth birthday. And while I possess grave doubts that she will appreciate a box now replete with approximately two dozen moist peach pits, I am not sorry to have prioritized my own survival over the happiness of her birthday.

My boredom is as profound as my hunger. I have been attempting to pass the time reading my fellow Colonists' letters. Yet another violation of my own Postal Code, which promises that all such missives remain private, but desperate times have driven me to curiosity. The correspondences tend to be a mixture of the banal (Elizabeth Clinton's churn is in such disrepair that her butter has been as lumpy as Martha Washington's cheeks) and the sordid (I had not a clue that Matthew Arbuckle rather enjoys when women to whom he is not betrothed take turns poking his inner thigh with the blunt end of a musket).

But even this diversion cannot last past this evening, as tomorrow will be Monday and this Philadelphia branch of the US Post Office will reopen for business after the Sabbath's respite. At that time, I shall attempt to escape and amend my already sullied legacy. Whereas I am currently Benjamin

BENJAMiN FRANKLIN

Franklin: Founding Father, statesman, inventor, printer, author, politician, scientist, musician, philosopher, and entrapped septuagenarian, tomorrow I hope to be Benjamin Franklin: Founding Father, statesman, inventor, printer, author, politician, scientist, musician, philosopher, and fleeing fugitive.

The question, my dears Ike and Claire Wanzandae, is where I will go upon exiting the confines of this structure. After hours of anguished vacillation, I have arrived at the conclusion that I will seek refuge on the property of Josiah Lockheed—the proprietor of an Inn some distance from town. Given the ill-reputed Nature of the activities said to take place in his establishment, Josiah has little choice but to be a man prone to discretion. And thus, I am confident that he will keep my presence a secret if I provide him with sufficient incentive. By which I mean: Money.

So therein lies my decision, Ike and Claire Wanzandae. At morrow's early light, I shall deposit this letter addressed to you in an Outgoing mail bin with every confidence that it will find you in the year in which you live, and then disguise myself by donning a postal carrier's uniform, exiting among the others, and furtively making my way to Josiah's.

I am,
Benjamin Franklin

CHAPTER 6

I read BF's letter and felt the gigantic balloon of terror in my chest deflate. He was alive, and I was a genius for figuring out to look in his mailbox for mail. Which I admit does not look like a rocket-surgeon-level thought on Paper, but still I felt pretty Unstoppable to be standing there in Proper attire with a bona fide road map to B-Freezy's whereabouts in hand when less than an hour earlier, if I had been a cartoon, the thought bubble over my head would have read "Buh?"

Now the thought bubble was full of exclamation points, like !!!!!!, because the name Josiah Lockheed was Known to me. He was the hallowed forebearer my butt-sandwich of a stepfather, Dirk the Jerk, was always bragging about and showing me old letters from, usually after he had Imbibed two or three beers and run out of boring Tales to tell my mom while she washed the dishes and he did nothing to Help even though she had also cooked the meal, which is exactly the type of inconsideration she used to get mad at my father for, but somehow The Jerk gets a free pass.

I had mostly paid Scant attention to the adventures of Josiah the Jerk, because a) it wasn't like he was *my* old-timey innkeeping ancestor, so who cares? and b) I had pretty much trained my Mind to switch channels whenever Dirk the Jerk started talking, and start replaying basketball highlights or counting to one million by sevens or whatever until he went Away. But I did know this much: anybody whose family line had Resulted in Dirk the Jerk had to have something wrong with him.

It didn't sound like BF trusted Josiah the Jerk—more like he considered him a shady enough customer that his silence could be bought. But the thing is: if you are a dude whose silence can be bought, your nonsilence can also be bought, because caring about money is the opposite of caring about loyalty.

That seemed pretty obvious to me, and I'm not exactly a criminal mastermind, as you may recall from such previous life occurrences as "Ike Sneaks Out At Night And Ends Up In Police Custody." So the next thought to barge into my head was: Maybe three days of sleeping on a countertop and eating nothing but peaches and brushing his teeth with glue has resulted in BF not being in tip-top mental Form. Maybe his judgment is impaired.

And hot on that thought's heels was that I had to find myself a Means of Transport posthaste, and get to the Inn before Josiah the Jerk ratted Ben Franklin out.

But how? Even if I figured out where the Inn was, I would need a stealthy and discreet way of getting there, so as not to Alert our enemies. A bike might work, if bikes existed. Except that if they did, I didn't have any money to buy one. And if they didn't, I didn't have time to invent them.

Also, I didn't know how, which was kind of a depressing thing to realize. Thinking that you're some kind of super smarty-pants who's going to crush the game and just casually invent a couple billion dollars' worth of inventions is one of the Pitfalls of traveling back in time. I mean, a bike isn't a nuclear reactor. It's about as simple a machine as there is. And I use one basically every day. But could I actually invent it? Probably not. The same thought had also crossed my mind about: the television, the basketball, the compass, and the nail gun. The garlic press, I might be able to invent. A whole bunch of board games, probably.

Suddenly, it came to me. I knew what I needed. Only it wasn't a what. It was a Who.

I needed the kid Ben had written about in his letter about fleeing the angry mob and getting to the Post Office. I needed the Young Scamp.

He had a horse and buggy. And he'd saved Ben once. Why wouldn't he do it again? Plus, he was a Daring Lad who knew his way around and didn't mind breaking the law if necessary.

With a speed born of Purpose, I marched back to Old Man Allerton's store. It was dark and empty, and about twenty degrees cooler than outside.

"Mr. Allerton?" I called. "Hello? It's me, Ike. Ben Franklin's friend."

He poked his head out of the stockroom. "Is there some problem with your purchases?" he asked. "For here at Allerton and Son Fine Garments for Men and Boys, we guarantee all craftsmanship in full for no less than six—"

"No, no," I assured him. "My garments are, um, Commendable. I need your help with something else." I stepped up to the counter, took off my hat, and thumped it down in a Serious fashion. "It's about Ben," I said in a low voice of Supreme Purpose.

Old Man Allerton's eyes got wide and he nodded. "Anything I can do, I shall," he whispered.

I was tempted to just ask Old Man Allerton to lend me a horse and buggy, since he was acting so down with Team Ben. But I figured he'd say one of two things: No, or Let me come. And as legit as he seemed, I didn't need some four-hundred-year-old Garmenteer horning in on my rescue mission. I needed somebody young and quick with Questionable morals. In my mind, the Young Scamp was looking more and more like Han Solo, which I guess made me Chewbacca. But that was fine. I like Chewbacca. Anybody who can get away with walking around nude except for an ammunition belt is pretty rad in my book.

"I need to find a horse and buggy thief," I said. "He rescued Ben from the mob. If I can find him, I think I can find Ben."

From the way Old Man Allerton's cheeks reddened in Consternation, I knew excluding him had been the right decision.

"What is the rapscallion's name?" he sputtered.

"I don't know. Ben calls him the Young Scamp."

"So he is youthful."

"Yeah. And scampy."

That made me think of shrimp scampi, which is

delicious. Maybe that was something I could invent, once the future of the Republic was secure.

"Hmm." Old Man Allerton stroked his whiskers. "The Middlebrookses' youngest son, Norman, has of late been confounding his parents with various acts of petty thievery. I wonder if he might be the scamp in question."

That was good enough for me, even if Norman Middlebrooks wasn't exactly the most swashbuckling of names. Then again, neither was Franklin Isaac Saturday. Plus, what was swashbuckling, anyway? If it involved buckling a swash, what was a swash? Or maybe you *made* the swash buckle, the way people's knees buckled in books. In which case, a swash was probably an old-timey word for a knee.

"Where can I find him?" I asked.

"One moment. I shall consult my ledger." Old Man Allerton opened a thick book and traced a column of names and addresses with his finger.

"The Middlebrookses' house is situated two blocks south and one and a half blocks east of this establishment, at Thirty-Three Lancaster Avenue. I cannot say whether young Master Norman might be found there, of course, but—"

I was already headed for the door. "Thanks, Mr. Allerton," I called over my shoulder. "Catch you later, okay?"

CHAPTER 7

Thirty-Three Lancaster Avenue was a big white house surrounded by a little white fence surrounded by little white roses. It didn't look anything like Ben Franklin's crib, in the sense that it was still standing rather than burned to the ground. I took a second to compose myself—not in the sense of calm myself, but in the other sense of compose, the one that means *make something up*, and then I whammed the brass knocker thing against the door. I wondered if BF had invented it. Seemed like something he would do.

A couple seconds passed, and then a brown-haired, freckle-faced kid a couple of years younger than me opened the door. He was wearing a thin white undershirt, and leather suspenders, and he had a gnawed-up corncob in his hand and corn all over his face.

"Who are you?" he said, and tossed the corncob onto his own front lawn.

"My name is Luke," I said. "Luke Skywalker. I'm looking for my friend Ben." I spread my legs, and shoved my hands into the pockets of my pantaloons, or whatever the heck I was wearing on my lower Limbs. "Ben *Franklin*," I added, with Gravity.

The kid just stared at me for a couple of seconds, like he was trying to figure out his next move. Then he said, "Who's Ben Franklin?"

That seemed suspicious, since BF was basically the most famous person in the entire city.

I took a step closer, feeling Emboldened by his answer. Also, this kid was a pipsqueak. His arms were like pipe cleaners. I could probably intimidate him. And if he turned out not to be the Young Scamp, maybe I could at least score a delicious piece of corn.

"I'm looking for the horse thief who took Ben to the Post Office," I said in the low, cool voice of a Hero. "And I think it was you."

The Possible Young Scamp picked a corn kernel out of his teeth with a dirty fingernail. "What's a horse?" he said.

On one hand, that was pretty Scampy. On the other, it

was pretty annoying. I decided the thing to do was apply some reverse psychology. Mom used to pull that on me when I was little, like by telling me I couldn't have any broccoli in order to make me want broccoli, although clearly the Young Scamp was a much cooler customer than I had ever been, even if his name was Norman.

I made a Show of looking him up and down, then said, "Sorry, my mistake. There's no way a lad as frail and puny as you could ever steal a horse, much less a buggy. Have a nice day." And I turned my back and started walking away, very slowly.

I was halfway to the front gate when the Young Scamp cried out in a shrill and Angry voice.

"I have stolen more horses than you have blemishes on your fleshy, paste-colored posterior!"

I turned back, and smiled.

"I thought so."

"I care not what you think, young Master Skywalker. What kind of foolish name is that, anyway?"

I ignored his last Remark, and said, "It just so happens that I am in need of a horse and buggy. And a skilled driver."

"What concern of mine is that? I am not a driver for hire." The Young Scamp puffed out his chest until I could see his ribs pressing against his shirt. "I am a criminal."

"That's why I'm here. A criminal is exactly what I'm looking for."

The Young Scamp descended the steps and sauntered down the walk to meet me. "And why is that, Skywalker?"

"Because Ben Franklin is hiding out in a wretched den of scum and villainy." That was Obi-Wan Kenobi's line about the Mos Eisley Cantina, and I felt bad mixing my Luke with my Obi-Wan, but whatever. The Young Scamp would never know.

I saw his eyes light up, and decided it was time to seal the deal.

"Make your decision quickly," I said. "You are not the only Young Scamp in town."

"I shall do it," the Young Scamp declared. "Follow me. I have a large selection of horses and buggies hidden down yonder, by the river basin."

"Excellent," I said. "But first, we need provisions. Go back inside, and grab all the food you can Muster."

The Young Scamp scampered up the stairs and disappeared into the house. A few minutes later, he reemerged with a Sizable basket dangling from his thin arm.

"I am ready if you are, Skywalker," he said.

"Then let us go and fight for the Future of this land," I said, and marched purposefully into the street as though I had some idea which way to Go.

CHAPTER 8

Josiah the Jerk's inn was called the Inn 'N' Out, and the Young Scamp knew exactly where it was located. He went there quite regularly, as it turned out, to sell stolen horses, buggies, and items found In stolen buggies, such as canes, bonnets, and whiskey, to both Josiah the Jerk himself and the Inn 'N' Out's clientele.

"'Tis a most unsavory place," he told me for the fourth or fifth time, cracking his whip against the flanks of our cloven-hooved employee, Butterscotch. "Mr. Franklin must truly be desperate, to keep the company of such scofflaws."

"He and I both," I mumbled.

"If you mean to offend me, you have failed," he replied. "There is more honor in a day of theft than in a year of politics."

"Whatever you say, Young Scamp," I said to the Young Scamp, who had informed me that he preferred Young Scamp to Norman. "So Josiah is, what, kind of a jerk, or . . . ?"

"I do not know this word," he said, glaring across the reins at me. "Truly, you do speak a most peculiar dialect. Where did you say you were from?"

"New Jersey."

He made a face like he had smelled something Unpleasant, possibly New Jersey, and said, "That explains it." A moment later, he continued. "Josiah is clever. Where other men see rules, he sees opportunities. To break those rules. And profit by it. I quite admire him, actually. Though if by 'jerk' you mean that he will yank you by the neck until you lie dead on the floor for the meagerest of reasons, then yes. He is a jerk."

"Yikes," I said, feeling my stomach curl into a ball like a frightened porcupine.

The Young Scamp shot me a look of Alarm. "There's no need for such language!" he said.

"Sorry," I said, and fell quiet.

To the left and to the right was moonlit countryside. The air was cool and smelled of hay and smoke, and besides the clop-clopping of Butterscotch, all I could hear was the occasional Hoot of an owl. I had been eager to get going, but the Young Scamp had insisted we wait until dark, as two kids driving alone were likely to Arouse suspicion, and we could not afford to do that.

So here we were, crossing through fields dotted with tiny houses, everybody inside probably fast asleep and planning on rising at the first rooster call to till the fields and milk the cows and whatnot. It was surprising how quickly Philly had opened up into farmland, and even more surprising how long we had been Traveling. I'd assumed that Josiah the Jerk's place would be close to the city, since generally you find the highest concentration of people and thus sleazebuckets in cities. But maybe Isolation had its benefits as well. Such as nobody knowing what you are up to.

Then we rounded a bend, and boom. There it was, looming in the distance: huge and wide, so white it glowed in the darkness, with dozens of windows illuminated by oil lamps. The whole place seemed to grin. I could hear noises inside: low voices and high ones, laughter and piano music and tinkling glass.

I rode toward it with my heart thumping in my chest, hoping that a) BF was there, and b) I wasn't about to screw things up even worse.

CHAPTER 9

Dear Claire Wanzandae,

First of all, let me apologize for not writing back sooner. I know you asked me to, and the last thing I want to do is make you worry, which I am sure I must have done because it's been a week since your letter came and maybe you are thinking I have been reduced to Atomic Dust. Not a day has gone by when I have not thought about you, and not just "I ought to write to Claire," but also "Man, do I miss Claire," and "I wonder what Claire is doing," and, I will admit, "I wish I was smelling the cherry-blossom-and-gasoline scent of Claire's long, beautiful hair right now."

The reason I have not written is that I have been too busy trying to survive. Maybe that sounds extreme, but I assure you, Claire Wanzandae, I am not exaggerating. And boy, do I have a new level of Perspective on what I considered to be problems back in the good old twenty-first century. Because stuff like "Am I Popular?" definitely pales in comparison to stuff like "Are The Dudes With Pitchforks Going To Recognize Us Despite Our Disguises?" But I am getting ahead of myself, so let me Rewind.

When I got your letter, I resolved to meet Ben at the inn he was fleeing to, which if you can believe it is owned by Dirk the Jerk's some-number-of-greats-grandfather, Josiah the Jerk—"Jerk" being a family Trait. Acting with the type of Quick Thinking Intelligence for which I am not known, but for which I would like to be known, I managed to locate the horse thief known to BF as the Young Scamp (real name: Norman Middlebrooks), and convince him to drive me there.

The Young Scamp, Claire Wanzandae, turns out to be approximately eleven years old. He is built like a crayon, but if he were a crayon his color would be Unimpressed, as in Color Me Unimpressed. Kids definitely grew up faster in Colonial times than they do in our day. Then again, a horse is a lot easier to hot-wire than a car.

My meeting with Ben was like something out of a movie, or a really exciting old-time book, so I am going to try to write it for you that way. All this letter-jotting and diary-keeping is making me think that maybe I would like to be a writer when I grow up, so I might as well get in some practice on things like Action and Dialogue right now. Maybe when I am back in the present we can sit down and go over these letters and you can tell me which parts were Pulse-Pounding Excitement and which parts were Snoozarific. I promise not to take offense if you say something is Snoozarific, because one thing about me that you should know is I am actually good at taking constructive criticism, Claire Wanzandae.

So picture it: night has settled over the farming towns outside Philly like a starry Blanket as the Young Scamp and I approach Josiah's inn, the Inn 'N' Out, which is lit up and full of people, and you can hear the sounds of laughter and music from a hundred yards away, even over the sound of hooves and the noise of the buggy bumping up and down on its primitive wheels, which do not have Shocks and consequently leave your butt feeling like you've been hit repeatedly with a baseball bat, except that baseball has not been invented.

"Is there anything I should know, before we go into the Inn 'N' Out?" I asked the Young Scamp.

He nodded. "There is one rule, and that rule is Do Not Provoke Josiah. His word is law here. I have seen him throw men out of the inn for daring to question him. Nor does he refund their money, should they be ejected before the service for which they paid has been rendered. And these are not men who are wanting in courage. On the contrary, these are men whom most would cross the street to avoid."

"Why are they afraid of him?" I asked. "Is he that tough?"

"Josiah won the inn in a game of cards," the Young Scamp informed me. "Before that, he was a . . . seafaring man."

"Like a pirate?"

The Young Scamp nodded his small, narrow head. "But I would not use that word in his presence, unless it is your wish to learn how far you can be tossed."

"It is not," I said.

"Perhaps it is best that I do the talking," said the Young Scamp. "One outlaw to another."

It was not good for my Ego to allow an eleven-year-old to put me in my place, Claire Wanzandae. But a lesson I have learned is that my Ego should not always get to run the show. After all, It is what made me act like such a toolbox that night on the playground when I expelled the contents of my stomach on you. So I nodded my head and told the Young Scamp that I agreed.

We parallel parked Butterscotch in a space between two other horse 'n' buggies and walked into the Inn 'N' Out. The contrast between the general Mood here and in Philly was striking, even if one was not so far from the other. Here, the mood was basically "Party On, Dudes And Dudettes" with no regard to the scandal and coming invasion that everyone was concerned about in Philadelphia.

A woman in a fancy dress was playing a Jaunty song on the piano, and about three dozen men and women were standing around, drinking and talking, in a gigantic room with high ceilings and two staircases leading up to the second floor.

"Where's Josiah?" I whispered to the Young Scamp, but as soon as I said it I felt foolish because striding toward us was a large man with long black hair and a shiny silver cutlass dangling off his belt.

"Good evening, Jos—" said the Young Scamp. Then he stopped speaking, because he could no longer draw air into his lungs. That was because his windpipe had been restricted, and that was because Josiah the Jerk had clamped a large, powerful hand around the base of his neck. The Young Scamp's feet kicked at the air. This was because they were no longer touching the ground, and this was because Josiah the Jerk was holding him up to his own scar-covered face, which was located at an Altitude several feet above the Young Scamp's natural location.

"Ya got a lotta nerve comin' around my place o' business, ya thievin' little thief," Josiah the Jerk growled in a voice I can only describe, Claire Wanzandae, as extremely piratelike.

I looked around for help, but no one seemed to care that a small boy was being strangled. Maybe the Inn 'N' Out's patrons were as rough-and-tumble as the owner. Or maybe they didn't care for the Young Scamp either.

He was shaking his head now, back and forth, and turning scarlet. His mouth was moving, but he couldn't speak.

"Put him down!" I cried out, and immediately clamped my hand over my mouth in horror at what I had done, for now the pirate was glaring down at me.

"Who in the wild blue yonder are you?" he asked, still holding the Young Scamp aloft. "What is this place becomin', a home fer maraudin' little crumbsnatchers?"

"We're here on business!" I declared. "Now please, release the Young Scamp before you kill him."

Josiah the Jerk stared at me with Murder in his eyes. Actually, just one of them. The other eye was glass, and it was looking in another direction Entirely.

"Business," he repeated, and unclenched the hand that held the Young Scamp, who dropped to the ground like a sack of laundry, if a sack of laundry could cough loudly. "The last time this accursed scofflaw brought his 'business' here, he absconded with two horses and a carriage belongin' to me finest customer."

The Young Scamp sat up, and managed to choke out some words. "I sold you the horse and buggy in which I came. I had to get home somehow."

"A smart answer from a foolish lad," Josiah the Jerk roared, and pulled out his cutlass. "I oughta cut a smile into yer throat and let yer blood water me begonias an' the like."

Acting with the type of Quick Thinking Intelligence for which I am not known, combined with the type of Not Fully Considering The Consequences Of My Words for which I am very well known, I blurted, "Do that, Josiah, and you will lose out on a ton of money."

His head swiveled toward me, and he raised his left eyebrow about three feet into the air. "How's that?" he inquired.

I summoned all the wits and daring I had In me, and said, "In a short while, a very wealthy and famous friend of mine is going to show up here and offer you a fortune to hide in one of your rooms. Unless, of course, I tell him not to."

"Which ye might have a bit o' trouble doin' if I slice out yer tongue," Josiah replied, sliding the flat, cold blade of the cutlass across my cheek. "But if the man ye mean is a certain disgraced diplomatic type, then ye be a day late and a doubloon short, says I. For the corpulent landlubber of whom ye speak is upstairs right now, gorgin' himself on potpies an' the like." And he pointed the cutlass at the staircase.

Josiah the Jerk saw the shock on my face, and grinned. From somewhere inside his shirt or vest or waistcoat or jacket, he removed a piece of paper, and showed me the signature at the bottom. It was Ben's.

"Feast yer eyes on this," he crowed. "'Tis the deed to your stringy-haired friend's house, which has now passed into my possession."

"But his house—" I began, and then realized that the next two words I was about to say were the two most idiotic and harmful words available to me at this moment in the entire English language, and stopped talking. Then, to Cleverly redirect his attention, I said, "Could you tell him that Ike's here?"

"I thought you said your name was Luke Skywalker," said the Young Scamp, who seemed to have regained his composure. Maybe being lift-choked was a more regular colonial Occurrence than I assumed.

"I thought you said Josiah the Jerk was a friend of yours," I shot back.

"Josiah the what?" said Josiah the Jerk.

"Josiah the Herc," I said. "Like Hercules. Because you're so strong."

Josiah the Jerk seemed to like that. "Indeed," he said, raising the cutlass to my cheek again. "Now what have ye ta say about the house of the man upstairs?"

"Me? Nothing. Can I see him now?"

Josiah the Jerk shook his head slowly from side to side. "I mighta been born on a Friday," he said, "but it wasn't last Friday. Ye said, 'But his house . . .' Now yer ta tell me the rest, or I'll decorate the drawin' room with yer entrails."

"Smells funny," I said. "That's what I was going to say. 'But his house smells funny.' Because he's old. And farts a lot."

"Yer eyes are full o' deceit," Josiah the Jerk said, and pressed the cutlass harder. "Give us the truth now, laddie, and be quick about it."

I'm not proud of this, Claire Wanzandae, but I told him the truth. I didn't want my entrails to decorate his drawing room.

"Burned down," I mumbled. "His house burned down."

A dark cloud passed over Josiah the Jerk's face, and

without another word he grabbed me by the neck and marched me up the stairs, then down a hallway and another, until at last we came to a closed door.

Josiah released me, and kicked it open.

Inside, lying on a bed with a full plate on his stomach, an empty plate by his side, and two more empty plates in the general vicinity of his feet, was a man I immediately recognized as my friend Benjamin Franklin.

He sprang to his feet more quickly than I would have imagined a man of his Girth could, sending the plate on his stomach clattering to the floor and the potpie that had Resided on it rolling underneath the bed. I made a mental note of its location, because it smelled delicious and I had eaten very little from the Young Scamp's picnic basket due to Nerves.

"What is the meaning of this intrusion?" Ben roared, his face red and small pieces of potpie flying from his mouth. He pointed a finger at me. "Who is this pint-sized interloper, and what kind of secrecy have I bought from you, Josiah Lockheed?"

"He says he's a friend o' yers," Josiah said, and pushed me into the room.

"Are you so softheaded that you would grant any scoundrel claiming to be my friend access to—"

You've Got Mail

"Ben," I said. "It's me. Ike. From the . . . letters."

He stopped talking, and the red drained out of his face, along with any other color that might have once resided there.

"Ike," he whispered. "It cannot be." Then he furrowed his brow, and stood a little straighter. "Prove it."

Being asked to prove that you are you is a weird thing, Claire Wanzandae. But I did not have much time to contemplate the Nature of the Self, because I knew that things were about to get very hairy very quickly in that room. So I kept it simple.

"You wrote me and Claire Wanzandae a letter asking for help," I said. "I think your exact words were 'HELP HELP HELP.' So here I am. Ready to help help help. My first suggestion is that we find a different place for us to put our heads together and figure out our next move."

Ben stepped forward and poked me—to see if I was real, I guess. Also real was the fingertip-shaped smudge of gravy he left on my tunic.

"The implications boggle the mind," he murmured, under his breath.

"As long as we're discussin' things that boggle the mind," Josiah the Jerk said, stepping forward until he was between BF and me, "how about me fist, slammin' against yer cantaloupe of a noggin? That oughta boggle it real good."

His hand shot out like a snake and grabbed Ben by the lapel of his jacket. "Seems ya neglected ta mention that the house ya sold me is a smokin' pile o' soot," Josiah the Jerk said.

"Where did you hear such—" Ben began, and then he stopped short, and looked over at me, and I felt my whole body burn with shame under the heat of his glare.

"It just slipped out," I said. "I'm sorry." I was trying not to cry or Soil my pants at the thought of what Josiah the Jerk was probably going to do next, such as: use his cutlass to slice us both into inch-long strips of Meat suitable for a stir-fry.

"It seems your definition of 'help help help' differs somewhat from mine," Ben said, in a surprisingly calm voice. Even more surprising was that it calmed me down, hearing it. It's hard to describe, Claire Wanzandae, but all of a sudden I kind of remembered: hey, this is *Benjamin Franklin*, and he is famous and Esteemed for a reason. He's got Wits, and he knows how to keep them even when he is being chased by a mob, or threatened by some dirtbag pirate. I felt my heartbeat slow down a little bit, like from Techno to Classic Rock.

"I have other assets, Josiah," he said, in a voice like a schoolteacher might use with a rowdy kid, a voice that was supposed to reclaim Control over the situation. "My name appears on over one hundred patents, for example. Any three of which I would be happy to sign over to you."

"Why?" Josiah the Jerk growled, tightening his grip on the cutlass until his knuckles whitened. "Have they burned down too?"

Ben chuckled. "The beauty of a patent is that it cannot burn down. It is eternal, as is the income that derives from it. And the credit. 'Josiah Lockheed, inventor of the bifocal'—has a nice ring to it, don't you think?"

Josiah the Jerk grimaced at him for a long moment, me tensing for calamity all the while, and then said, "Aye. That it does. And likewise 'Josiah Lockheed, inventor of the Glass Harmonica,' and 'Josiah Lockheed, inventor of the Franklin Stove.'"

"Henceforth to be known as the Lockheed Stove," BF said, smiling a Large smile and nodding his head fast and with false but convincing Enthusiasm.

Josiah the Jerk lowered his cutlass.

"I shall draw up a legally binding document this very eve," B-Freezy declared, straightening his rumpled clothing and walking over to a beat-up rolltop desk in the corner of the room and grabbing a quill. "Now, Josiah, if you please—might

I have a moment to confer with my young friend here? He comes bearing news of great import, I'm sure."

Josiah eyed us both, with a *You Better Not Try Any Funny Stuff*-type look, and then he said, "Aye," and backed out of the room and closed the door.

As soon as it clicked shut, Ben put down the quill he'd been messing with and speed-waddled over and locked the lock.

Then he threw the window open, pulled the top sheet off the bed, and started tying knots in it.

"What are you doing?" I asked, like a Moron. Because any moron could see that he was planning an exit, via a port of departure that was Not the door.

"I will be dead in the ground before I sign my greatest inventions over to that rank-smelling scofflaw." He shook his head at me, and narrowed his eyes. "I fear your journey has robbed you of whatever brainpower you possessed in your own epoch. Now hasten. Before that seafaring imbecile realizes I am no barrister."

He tied one end of the sheet to a bedpost, and threw the other out the window.

I will write a Part Two of this letter as soon as possible, Claire Wanzandae, but right now I am out of parchment and also very Low on ink. But do not worry. I am OK. Or, if not

OK, then at least alive and fighting the good Fight, whatever that means.

Thinking of You Very Much,
Ike

CHAPTER 10

From the Journal of Benjamin Franklin

For all the years of my life, I have faithfully kept a journal, and so I continue to do so even now, when all that I was has fallen Away. I may have lost my reputation, my home, even my Understanding of science (for it is Science, and the Postal System I invented, which has conspired to deliver Franklin Isaac Saturday to my doorstep, though I use the term *doorstep* figuratively, as a doorstep is yet another thing I no longer Possess), but I shall remain faithful to my habit of inscribing the Events of the day into a journal whenever I may. It is for this reason, in fact, that I had the presence of mind to steal a leather-bound guest book from Josiah Lockheed's inn. It is this in which I write at Present. I might even say that writing in this book is the only thing that keeps me sane, as Ike and I endeavor to stay alive in the rural countryside of Pennsylvania, but I shall get to that in Time.

First, an accounting of our initial Escape, together with my first Impression of the lad who styled himself my Savior.

He is a great deal smaller than I had imagined he would be. While nothing in our correspondence had indicated the quantity of flesh attached to the frame of this letter writer from the future, my presumption was that it might match the enormous breadth of his pluck. Instead, much to my befuddlement, he possesses not the physique of a strapping young lad but rather that of an inconsequential street urchin.

My second impression—ascertained while I was busy tying a bedsheet to a bedpost so that I might Shinny to safety before Josiah Lockheed realized I had deceived him a second time and returned to gut me like a trout—was that Ike was as Annoying in person as he was in letters.

As I was attempting to clamp my Ample legs around the means of Escape, he interrupted with the following:

"Whoa, B-Freezy! Shouldn't I be the first to go down that sheet?"

"Pray tell, why?" I responded, in case his reason was less Foolish than everything else about him had thus far Proven to be.

"Because I'm your guest. I'm the one who traveled. In baseball the Visiting team always bats first. It's a courtesy that hosts extend to the people they've invited."

As a statesman and diplomat who has made the acquaintances of men and women in both the American colonies and in a number of European nations, I was now certain that I could say without fear of contradiction that I was dealing with the most irritating specimen of humanity on either side of the Atlantic.

"Firstly," I responded, "you were not invited. In point of fact, you simply arrived, unannounced, of your own volition."

"What's secondly?" he then asked.

"Why do you presume there is a secondly?"

"Well, people don't say 'firstly' unless it's going to be followed by a 'secondly.' Otherwise, they just say whatever they want to say and get on with their lives."

At this point, though I have never been to the continent of Asia, I was now certain that I was dealing with the most irritating specimen of humanity on either side of the Pacific. So I plumbed the depths of my considerable vocabulary to avoid uttering a word that was even remotely reminiscent of the word *secondly*.

"Furthermore—" I continued.

"Ooh, burn," he interrupted, an utterance I found both rude and unfathomable.

"I am attempting to, as you say, 'get on with my life' by fleeing this Inn," I went on. "By proceeding first, I eliminate the possibility of falling atop you, should my considerable weight cause this bedsheet to tear. Stand aside."

I then grabbed the end of the sheet and attempted to make my descent. At this point, the bedpost around which the sheet was knotted disengaged from the actual bed and took flight across the room, leaving by way of the very window from which I had exited mere moments earlier. I dropped to the ground in accordance with every postulate purported by Galileo in regard to falling objects, and was followed almost immediately by Ike, who landed on my stomach with a force that seemed incommensurate with his puniness.

"Okay!" said Ike, rolling off of me and springing to his feet as I struggled to draw air into my flattened lungs. "Let's make like a tree and leave!"

"Indeed," I gasped, for Josiah was now leaning out the window from which we had just Egressed, wielding his cutlass and shouting threats no less frightening for being unintelligible.

Desperately, I looked about for means of escape and espied a horse 'n' buggy. "Let us abscond with that carriage," I suggested, pointing.

"That's just what I was about to say," Ike informed me. "It's like we're thinking with one brain, BF."

"It would explain a lot," I muttered.

Ike frowned. "How do you mean?"

"If we share but one brain between the two of us,

that would explain why we are standing here like a pair of fools instead of effecting an escape." I looked up and saw that Josiah was no longer in the window, and therefore was most assuredly bounding down the Inn's stairs, cutlass in hand.

"Good point," said Ike. "And besides, this is the Young Scamp's horse 'n' buggy, which means that it's already stolen. It doesn't count as stealing if you're taking something that's already stolen."

His rationale was bereft of logic, but this was not a time for Socratic discussion as at that very moment the front door of the Inn 'N' Out burst open and out rushed Josiah.

"Fine," I answered, heaving my girth into the backseat.

To my surprise and further annoyance, Ike joined me there, leaving us very much without a driver.

"What are you doing?" I asked, though what I truly meant was *Why are you doing it*? "Take the reins."

"But I've never driven a horse 'n' buggy. In fact, I've never driven a horse 'n' anything."

"Neither have I," I offered in retort. "Did you

not travel here in order to provide help?"

"Yeah, but I was thinking I could help by providing, like, important knowledge from the future that would help us win the war."

"At the moment," I said, perspiring freely from both the fear of imminent dismemberment and the frustration of dealing with one so obtuse, "we are not in need of knowledge, but of velocity. Commence!" With that, I shoved Ike roughly toward the front of the carriage.

"Okay, whatever," he said sullenly. But he did pick up the reins, and to his credit, managed to convince the horse to commence galloping. A mere instant before Josiah and his cutlass reached us, we accelerated into the unknown void of the starry night.

CHAPTER 11

Dear Claire Wanzandae,

That night, we slept in a barn. If you have never slept in a barn, which I am guessing you have not, I would basically advise: don't. Sometimes in movies and whatnot you see people passing out in haylofts on top of a nice soft bale o' hay and it looks peaceful and cozy. But in real life, 1) barns smell like a combination of horses, cows, horse poop, and cow poop, and 2) hay is the itchiest, pokiest substance in the world. It also does not help if your sleeping companion is a diplomat who has recently eaten four to six Potpies and is under extreme stress, because sometimes stress can be expressed through the Digestive Tract, if you get my meaning.

I was asleep when we arrived, and it was all I could do to stumble into the barn and resume my Slumber, so it was not until an extremely uncool rooster woke me up at the first light of dawn that I was able to ask such questions as Whose barn is this? and Where can we find some food?

B-Freezy did not have a whole lot of answers. The barn did not belong to an ally or anything. He had pulled in there for the same reason you pull into a motel on a road trip: because you are too tired to drive any farther and they have FREE HBO! on the sign, except for the HBO part, and the sign part. Also, this was different from a motel in that we were not Welcome Guests, but squatters.

"Why didn't we just sleep in the buggy?" I asked.

"Because it is too small to allow more than one of us to assume a reclining position, and I cannot sleep sitting up," BF replied—kind of haughtily, considering that he had hay stuck to his face. He also had not shaved in probably a week, and his beard was coming in grayish-black and thick, which made him look both tough and homeless. At least one of which was true.

"Speaking of the buggy, where is the buggy?" I asked. "And did you feed the horse?"

"I parked it discreetly, some ways off," Ben said. "And yes. I gave him some apples I found in a bucket. Presumably

intended for these more capable and better-built quadrupeds."
He pointed at the three horses stabled in the barn.

"Maybe we ought to trade him for one of them," I suggested.

Ben's face reddened. "My résumé has already suffered
enough. I do not wish to add 'horse thief' to it."

"What about 'horse trader'?"

"Enough insolence. Gather your limited wits and let us be
on our way, before the owner of this barn comes out to milk
his cows." He turned and started toward the door.

"You could have saved an apple or two for me," I said.

Ben turned, and frowned at me. "Do you intend to pull
the buggy?"

"No."

"Then your sustenance is no priority of mine."

That was a pretty mean thing to say, but I didn't respond
because I was tired of fighting. To be honest, Claire Wanzandae,
I was feeling pretty demoralized. The BF I knew from letters
could be gruff, sure. Maybe even obnoxious. But he was
also affectionate, at least once in a while. Throughout our
correspondence, I always felt like he and I were friends. Or if
not friends, maybe family, a grandfather and grandson—because
with family you can squabble and argue and be jerky, but you are
still Bound together. But ever since I'd gotten here, I hadn't felt

any of that warmth. BF seemed to see me as nothing more than a burden, even though I had come here to help him. Even though I had left behind my own family and You, and mailed myself here without knowing whether I would even survive the trip. When a guy does something like that, he expects a little Credit.

Then again, these were stressful times, and to be fair I hadn't actually provided any Help yet. Mostly I had provided Spilling The Beans About The House And Almost Getting Ben Killed By A Pirate. So maybe he was right to be salty. I decided I would Earn his affection. I knew he had it in him.

So I just sighed, and hurried to catch up, which was not very hard because of his Propensity to waddle. In fact, I had time to first take a good look around for any Items that might be useful and thus worth Borrowing. I found a straight razor among the assorted tools hung from the wall, and put it in my pocket, figuring that BF would welcome the opportunity to shave.

We exited the barn together, and soon were back on the road, as a rosy dawn bloomed ahead of us.

"We need food, disguises, and shelter," I pointed out helpfully.

Ben didn't answer.

"And we should name the horse," I said after a minute. "How about Lamborghini?"

You've Got Mail

Ben looked straight ahead, instead of over at me. "Whatever you say." And then, more silence, except for the rattle of the buggy and the clop-clopping of Lambo's hooves.

"Also," I added, in a kind of *yay, teamwork!* voice, "we should come up with a supercool plan."

That got me a look. It also got Ben's face glowing red with Anger. "Listen here, you incorrigible little—"

"What's *incorrigible* mean?" I asked because I knew it would annoy him. Suddenly, that was what I wanted to do, Claire Wanzandae, because enough is Enough.

"It means incapable of improving oneself. As in 'the incorrigible little boy ignored the advice of his wiser, older friend and foolishly traveled backward in time.'"

"Uh, excuse me, but does this ring a bell? 'HELP HELP HELP.' That's what you said to me. 'HELP HELP HELP.'"

"The only reason I needed help help help is because of your meddlings. Your maps and sandwiches."

"Yeah, but you still needed help help help."

Ben said nothing, because he knew that was true.

I pressed my advantage. "I think you should apologize for being so rude to me ever since I got here. I could have died traveling through time, you know."

Now it was Ben's turn to sigh. "You are very brave," he

said. "That much I cannot deny. Perhaps my words have been overly harsh, young Master Ike."

It was the first nice thing he'd ever said to me outside a letter, and it made all the insults kind of melt away, at least temporarily. "It's cool," I said. "You're under a lot of stress. I know I'd be a wreck if everybody went from loving me to wanting to burn me alive."

Ben nodded, and for a second I thought he might even cry.

"We'll also need money," he said just above a whisper.

"Don't you have any? Don't they pay you for being a Founding Father, inventor, ambassador, and all of those other things you do so well?"

"Yes, but aside from the few coins in these pockets, I fear it's all gone."

"How?" I asked.

It couldn't have been by betting on sports, I figured, because most sports hadn't been invented yet, unless he bet on horseshoes.

"In the fire. When they burned down my house, all of my money went up in flames as well."

"You kept all of your money in your house?" I asked.

"Under my mattress—which I can only suspect was also consumed."

BF's suspicions were correct. I saw the remains of his onetime house. And unless his mattress had been made of granite—which could've been the case given his stooped posture—there's no way there was anything under the mattress ashes except for more ashes.

"I'm sorry," I said.

I was tempted to say "I'm sorry, B-Fire Drill," but I stopped short of doing so, figuring that we were making a connection here and I didn't want to risk ruining it with an ill-timed clever joke.

I looked at him. He looked sad. Hopeless. Defeated. In need of a hug that I didn't dare attempt because there was no way my arms could possibly reach around him and that thought might depress him more.

"If only there were some magical tonic that could reverse our fortunes," he said, staring out across the open plain.

The phrase *magical tonic* rattled around in my head for the next few minutes as we drove on. It reminded me of something. I didn't know what, but I had the feeling it was important. And then, all at once, it hit me, and I stood up full of excitement and nearly fell out of the carriage.

"I've got it!" I said. "I just came up with a plan."

An idea would have been more accurate. *A possibly terrible idea* would have hit the nail right on the head. Except that we had no hammer. A hammer would have been nice, Claire Wanzandae. Also some duct tape. A man feels more Secure with duct tape.

"To save our Nation To Be?" asked Ben, with a Hopeful look on his face.

"No," I said, sitting down. "To save us. We're going to need money for food and shelter if we're going to be in any condition to protect ourselves from not getting murdered by yokels first, and then we figure out how to save America second."

Ben gave me a grim look, but I could tell he was Swayed by the wisdom of my words. "I do not know what Yokels are, but I do not believe I want to be murdered by them, regardless. I am loath to even ask, but what is your plan?"

One thing you do not know about me, Claire Wanzandae, is that last year, in sixth grade, I did my big ten-page Research Project, which was 25 percent of our history grade for the whole semester and had to involve at least three sources, on: Medicine Shows.

More than likely, you are asking yourself *What is a Medicine Show?* You are not alone.

"What is a Medicine Show?" asked Benjamin Franklin.

"I'm glad you asked," I said. I was finally feeling useful,

the way a Lad of the Future is supposed to when he travels back in time. "The Medicine Show, which is not scheduled to be invented until the nineteenth century, is basically a way of scamming gullible hillbilly types out of their money by selling them fake miracle cures."

"That sounds highly unscrupulous," BF huffed.

"Totally. And as American as apple pie."

"I have never heard that saying."

"You can have it," I told him. "Now back to this Medicine Show thing. It's very simple. All we need is some bottles and something to put in them that won't kill people. Like alcohol. But mixed with something else. Like apple juice."

"And assuming we are able to obtain this nauseating concoction? What then?"

"Then we do a little song and dance."

"I neither sing nor dance."

"Also just an expression. We ride into town and dazzle the crowd with a presentation where we explain that this nauseating concoction was specially formulated by you, Dr. Hezekiah J. Fibbelstream, by combining an old Choctaw recipe with modern German science, and the result is a wondrous Tonic that cures insomnia, gout, hay fever, and polio, strengthens bones and teeth, improves vision and hearing, and increases intelligence and vigor. Or whatever. They line up to buy it, and we ride out of town before they figure out it's all a bunch of nonsense."

Ben was staring at me so hard I felt like he might bore a couple of holes in my head. "Have you not heard my famous maxim stating that honesty is the best policy?" he demanded.

"'All Sales Final' is the best policy," I answered. "And if you want to have a maxim battle, here's one for you: There's a sucker born every minute."

"Who authored that appalling phrase?"

"P. T. Barnum. Although he hasn't been born yet, I don't think."

BF thought about it for a moment, then said, "Desperate times call for desperate measures."

"That's one of yours?"

He shook his large, mountain-shaped head. "It is from the Latin. *Extremis malis extrema remedia.* The author may have been—"

"I don't actually care. How much money do you have on you?"

"Only a few meager coins."

"Will it buy us some bottles and something to put in them?"

"I daresay it might. But what of the more pressing matter

of disguise? Surely I cannot present myself as Dr. Hezekiah
J. Fibbelstream when my face is so recognizable and so—"

Ben gulped, as if trying not to cry.

"—so hated," he finished.

That, Claire Wanzandae, is when I showed BF the razor
I had borrowed from the farm. His eyes widened, and he ran
a hand over his scraggly beard. "I should think this growth
invaluable as a disguise."

"Absolutely," I said. "The beard stays. But we're going
to have to shave your head."

To be honest, I did not do a great job of shaving BF's head,
though mostly that was the razor's fault, since it was very dull
and also we had no shaving cream or any other lubricating
substance. By the time I was done, he had multiple nicks
and gashes all over his bald cranium with thin rivulets of
blood streaming from them, and between that and the beard
he looked pretty thoroughly deranged.

But also, he looked like Dr. Hezekiah J. Fibbelstream,
mad genius inventor of Fibbelstream & Grandson's Miracle
Apple Tonic. Especially after we located a farm stand and
purchased, with the last of Ben's money, seventeen bottles of
fresh-pressed apple juice from an eight-year-old girl and her
six-year-old sister.

We were in business, Claire Wanzandae. A business that was to completely destroy the Positive Vibes that were now circulating between me and BF, but I am getting ahead Of myself.

And as we have just come upon a rural Post Office, I am going to say Good-bye and mail this letter now. I am thinking of you Fondly, and I will continue this Tale as soon as I can get some more time to write.

Yours,
F.I.S.

CHAPTER 12

From the Journal of Benjamin Franklin

I abhor dishonesty. My hatred for false dealings is surpassed only by my hatred of my pigeon toes, which give the impression that my feet are walking away from each other.

The very concept of a "miracle cure" is as repugnant to me as the scabs forming on my head and neck, which are there thanks to a shave Ike saw fit to give me so that I might remain incognito during our forthcoming medicine show, a charlatan's attraction in which I have agreed to participate for one simple reason: I do not wish to starve to death.

"Okay, Gramps, what do you say we stop here and set up shop?"

My initial reaction was one of complete silence, as I looked around to see if Ike's grandfather had mailed himself back in time to the town we had just entered. A town that was small and ramshackle, replete with rickety houses, stores, tumbleweeds, and swirling billows of dust.

When I did not respond, the little imp elaborated with alacrity.

"You're Gramps," he said. "Get used to it. If I'm gonna pass myself off as Igbert, the grandson of Dr. Hezekiah J. Fibbelstream, you're gonna have to get used to answering to Gramps."

"Fine."

"Let's practice."

"No cause for rehearsal, Igbert," I replied, summoning every muscle in my being to restrain my hands from finding his neck and squeezing as hard as humanly capable. "I fully understand my role in this charade. Though I do not understand why you must be Igbert, as no one in this century knows your actual name."

You've Got Mail

"Look alive, Gramps! We've got a crowd!"

And indeed, I turned to look where he was pointing and espied a growing number of men and women who had apparently left the confines of their rickety abodes and were now drifting toward us with curious looks on their faces.

"Notice anything odd about them?" he asked. Or rather, that is what I believe he asked, as a noise in the street was mounting that made casual conversation a distinct improbability.

"May I trouble you to repeat your last inquiry?"

"Notice anything odd about them?" he repeated. Or at any rate, that it is what I believe he repeated, as the ambient din was growing louder. The noise bore semblance to a familiar sound: that of a colonist coughing. More accurately, that of two dozen colonists coughing concurrently. Upon shifting my gaze toward the source of this guttural cacophony, my conjecture was affirmed. The townsfolk of this unfortunate burg were, indeed, all coughing.

"Who are you people?" Ike inquired of the crowd, which continued to grow in number and volume.

"We live here," answered a member of the throng, who then resumed coughing.

"Forgive me for asking," Ike continued, "but my grandfather and I couldn't help notice that all of you are coughing. Is that some secret signal that you all have with each other? Like how bus drivers honk when they pass each other on the road?"

The crowd went silent, then uttered a collective chorus of the syllables "What?" and "Huh," and then immediately went back to coughing.

"Whoops, wrong century," Ike murmured to me before raising his voice and readdressing the crowd, which had by now formed a half circle in front of our buggy.

"So what's wrong with all of you?" he asked.

The man who had spoken earlier did so again.

"We do not know," he offered between dry heaves. "But all of us who work at the coal mine are so afflicted."

Ike raised his eyebrows and nodded. "Black lung," he whispered to me. "It's a disease you get from inhaling too much coal dust."

Why a rapscallion who had displayed not one

scintilla of useful knowledge about anything was aware of this particular affliction is, to this very moment, a mystery to me. However, he was as resolute in his diagnosis as I am in my assertion that it was I (and not two little old women who tied ice skates to the bottom of a chair in 1710) who invented the rocking chair.

"What is the cure for this insidious malady?" I inquired of him.

"There is none . . ." Ike said, as a diabolical smile spread across his visage, "until now!"

It was then that Ike lifted one of the seventeen bottles of fresh-pressed apple juice we had purchased, and proclaimed to the retching crowd, "Ladies and gentlemen! Help is here!"

"Tell us more!" they exclaimed as one.

"It's the invention of my grandfather, Hezekiah J. Fibbelstream!" Ike proclaimed, lifting my arm into the air. "Like all of you, he worked in a mine for many years. And like all of you, he was coughing all the time. So what did he do? He quit working in the mine, enrolled in the University of Pennsylvania . . ."

"Which I founded," I reminded him in a low voice.

". . . coughed his way through all four years, then coughed during all four years of medical school. And the day he graduated, *Doctor* Hezekiah J. Fibbelstream invented this miraculous cure-all tonic! As you can see before your very eyes, he has not coughed since."

Ike then cast his gaze in my direction, and I felt compelled to speak. Despite my new beard and the carnage that had made the top of my head look like a relief map of the Appalachians, I had been concerned that my fellow colonists might recognize me. But it was now clear that they did not, and so I resigned myself to playing my role.

"It is true," I lied through my heretofore honest teeth. "Every word."

"You see?" Ike, or perhaps I should say Igbert, continued. "We've been traveling from one coal-mining town to another curing coal-mining folks of the same disease you have. That's why we only have seventeen bottles left. Seventeen bottles that we sold to everyone else for two dollars apiece. But because we like you guys way better than those other coughers, you can have the rest of our supply for the bargain-basement price of one dollar per bottle."

As a man who has now inhabited this great planet for threescore and ten years, I employ a regimen to stave off the inevitable ravages of advancing age. For example, it was not long ago that I would partake of four hearty meals a day and then, upon completion of each, walk jauntily along the streets of my beloved Philadelphia to aid and abet all processes of metabolism and convert consumed fats into units of energy. But now, in deference to the weakened state of those joints located in my knees and hips, I no longer walk jauntily. I simply walk. I have also switched to seven hearty meals a day.

And apparently this regimen has succeeded in preserving the keen mind that yours truly is renowned for, as I can recall with distinct clarity the moment the last bottle was sold to an eager black-lunged miner. For at that moment, Ike slapped the posterior of the swaybacked mare that had brought us there and we departed the rickety town square in less time than it took George Washington of Virginia to concoct his fictitious story about chopping down that infernal cherry tree to prove he did not lie.

* * *

When we had put an ample amount of distance between ourselves and that town, we halted our forward progress to allow the quadruped to cool down, and for Ike and I to reconnoiter.

"We now have exactly seventeen dollars," he announced with glee. "That's probably like seventy-five million in my year. We could buy our own plane if they'd been invented."

"I did not enjoy that," I said. "Although I gather that you did."

"*Extremis malis extrema remedia*, Hezekiah."

I did not respond. If this was what was required of me in order to stay alive, so that I might still pull our fledgling country back from the brink of Ruin, I would do it. But I would not do it gladly. Nor would I pretend to. I could feel my resentment toward Ike increasing, for forcing me to be complicit in this chicanery. I confess that this was not fair, and that I should have tempered my feelings with an acknowledgment that he had indeed kept us from starving to death or being recognized and murdered. But alas, I failed to summon such equanimity, and instead our relationship continued to deteriorate, even as we played at being family.

All that week, Dr. Fibbelstream and Igbert visited unsuspecting town after unsuspecting town, and presented our bottled apple juice as a wondrous elixir to the desperate and gullible. It was a carefree, easy life, except for the constant fear of being discovered as a fraud, apprehended, and having my four limbs tied to four horses who would then be instructed to run in four different directions. The fact that I was equally likely to suffer this fate as both the fraudulent Dr. Hezekiah J. Fibbelstream and the disgraced Founding Father Benjamin Franklin bore heavily upon my heart. But I did come to enjoy sleeping illicitly in barns and cooking my nightly repast over an open fire. Some spirit of adventure had been rekindled in me, I confess, by this preposterous and immoral ruse. But overall, I had never been more miserable.

For even with this newly discovered zest for life, I could not enjoy my freedom. In every waking moment and with every cough-free breath, I dwelled upon the impending doom of my beloved nation, my thirteen colonies, as conditions appeared to be getting worse.

"Conditions Getting Worse!"

The headline of the *Philadelphia Gazette* confirmed every fear I harbored. And while I was not afforded the opportunity to read any more of the newspaper, as it was being used to cover the mouth of a coal miner waiting to purchase the purported panacea Ike and I were selling and it billowed out every time he coughed, my thoughts, once again, turned inward. Bemoaning the personal state of affairs that saw me peddling false hopes and apple juice when my Nation-to-be and my city of residence were suffering the renewed and redoubled oppression of the British crown already was more than I could bear. I resented my fate, and I despised Dr. Hezekiah J. Fibbelstream. But after a week of Medicine Shows, sometimes as many as three a day, what I hated most of all was the doctor's loudmouthed, unscrupulous, and silver-tongued grandson, that vile young ignoramus known as Igbert.

"Yo, B-Freezy," he piped up on the eighth morning

of our sojourn together, which seemed to me more like the eightieth, as we set out in our buggy in search of more colonists to connive out of their hard-earned coin, "you seem kind of down. What's got your woolen pantaloonies in a bunch, dude?"

In that instant, I felt all my discontents surging, flowing like rain-engorged rivers from my heart and my head toward my mouth. The loss of my reputation. The failure of our mighty Declaration, over which the finest if most intermittently irritating minds of my generation had worked so hard. The reduction of my domicile to a smoldering pile of ash. The fact that I had not consumed a decent potpie in nearly a fortnight.

"Conditions Getting Even Worse!" proclaimed the headline of the *Gazette's* next edition being read by a coughing customer at our next stop, and at this point, all rivers of my growing discontent converged, and I unleashed a flood of words at the person whom I held responsible for it All.

"Are you really so daft as to ask me that question?" I roared, so loudly that our beast of burden took it upon himself to cease perambulating and looked back at me with an expression of glassy-eyed wonder. "I can pinpoint the beginning of all my woes. It is the day I received your first infernal letter! You are a curse upon me, Franklin Isaac Saturday! How I wish I had never invented the Post Office that delivered your missives, your Claireikes, your maps, or your Person into my life!"

I stopped, and braced myself for an equally impassioned retort. The force of my words had inflamed me, and I had an urge to loosen my garments so that the heat of my body might escape.

But rather than responding in kind, as Thomas Jefferson of Virginia or John Adams of Massachusetts would have, my companion burst into tears.

I allowed him to cry for some Minutes, not because I took any pleasure in the sight but because I did not know what to do. It has been many a year since I have been called on to soothe the emotions of a young boy. Particularly one whose upset I have caused by accusing him of destroying my life and country.

When he had stanched the flow of tears, Ike looked at me, blinked away some residual moisture, and said, "Why are you so mean to me? I'm only trying to help."

You've Got Mail

"Your help is what got me here," I informed him. I could feel my anger beginning to recede, but this was the moment to make my position clear, so I forced myself to remain unbowed with every wish that my lower body could do the same so I wouldn't always look like I was riding an invisible horse.

"I do not doubt your intentions, Ike," I went on, in an attempt to be both judicious and firm. "But this is not a partnership I ever sought. You are not without your good qualities, such as . . ." —and here I racked my overtaxed brain, beneath its poorly shorn cranium—"such as a true talent for defrauding country bumpkins, and . . . an admirable horsemanship and . . . passable personal hygiene. But it now appears that things have gotten worse in my City of Brotherly Love, so the time has come to part ways. I must return to Philadelphia and do what I can to save my country, or die trying. You must take me there, and then return to whatever is left of the future."

Again, the lad was quiet for a disturbing length of time.

Finally, he said, "But I saved your life."

"On the contrary, I can think of several ways in

which you have come close to getting me killed."

"What about Dr. Fibbelstream? I kept you safe—"

"Not yet murdered by former admirers who now loathe my existence is not the same as safe."

"—and made you a fortune."

"Perhaps I can use it to buy a new house to replace the one that burned down thanks to your meddling."

We stared balefully at each other. Lamborghini was polite enough to turn away.

"You were my hero," said Ike, in an accusing Tone. "I looked up to you."

"Then we have disappointed each other," I said, beginning to feel as forlorn as he appeared. "I had hoped none would look down on me until I lay in my coffin. But then I had also hoped to be a Founding Father, not a hated fugitive in my own city. We do not always get what we wish for."

"Maybe you should write that down in your stupid book of stupid sayings," Ike replied, and turned our horse around. "I thought we were friends, but I guess I was wrong."

I felt his anguish in that moment, and had the urge to assure him that despite it all, we were indeed friends. But, I am ashamed to say, my pride intervened, as it so often has in this long life of mine, and I remained silent.

"You know what? It's not my fault you morons spilled jelly on the Declapendence, and it's not my fault you morons didn't check before you gave it to the printer. Heck, with Founding Fathers like you, it's no wonder the country is as screwed up as it is. Maybe we're better off staying a British Colony after all."

His words cut me to the quick. They were no less mean-spirited for being true. My apology froze on my lips, and instead I sputtered, "You don't really mean that."

He had given me a taste of my own medicine. Or perhaps my own medicine show. Was it I, Benjamin Franklin—Founding Father, statesman, inventor, printer, author, politician, scientist, musician, philosopher, and creator of the postal system—who had taught this Youth to speak with such venom? Perhaps it was.

But now a great chasm lay between us, and I felt helpless to ford it.

We did not speak all the way to Philadelphia.

CHAPTER 13

I am not going to lie. I had not traveled all the way back in time, at great peril and without knowing if I would even Make it, just to be insulted repeatedly and told I was unwelcome by the very guy who had begged me for help.

Maybe I haven't talked about it much, but my life is pretty severely lacking in the department of: Father Figures. I mean, my actual father is all the way across the country in California building movie sets and when we do talk on the phone he's always apologizing and trying to get me to understand the Necessity of his move, which I frankly do not, since there is no shortage of things to hammer nails into in Philadelphia. Dirk the Jerk's forehead, for example, is practically calling out for a good hammering. I would rather take my cues on Manhood from a warm cup of hamster urine than from Dirk the Jerk.

So I guess because of this Void, and through his letters and our adventures together, B-Freezy had become kind of like a grandfather to me—especially since that was exactly what he was pretending to be. A surly, arrogant grandfather who complained about everything and snored, but a grandfather Still. So when he unloaded on me like that, all I could think to do was unload right back. It didn't make me feel any better, let me tell you. In fact, it made me want to cry again. I wasn't used to crying. I'd felt like doing so a few times. Mostly when I got off the phone with my dad after he told me still another reason why he wouldn't be seeing me during Christmas or my birthday. But just like I wouldn't give Dirk the Jerk the satisfaction every time he was mean to me or my mom or Carolyn, I used my Will to force the tears back into my tear ducts, and clenched my jaw so tight my teeth started to ache (though that might also have been a result of No Toothpaste) and shut my mouth.

I decided I wasn't going to say another word until BF apologized. That turned out to be two whole agonizingly quiet and boring days, which is how long it took us to get back to the City of Brotherly Love traveling by means of Very Tired Horse. We now had money but no food, and since I wasn't talking to Ben and Ben had apparently decided to retaliate by not talking to me, neither of us was willing to admit we were hungry and stop to purchase some grub from a farm, which was what we'd mostly been doing in this land of No Restaurants. Instead we just drank up the last twelve bottles of Dr. Hezekiah J. Fibbelstream's Miracle Apple Tonic, which seemed kind of poetically tragic to me, for some reason. Especially when I drank part of one bottle down the wrong pipe and proceeded to cough like a coal miner for the next half hour.

Two days is a very long time to hold a grudge. All I could think about was going home. My life in 2015 had finally turned a corner and started to get good. I had Claire, who made junior high not just bearable but fun. And every day I was gone was a day my mom was probably worrying herself to death. If we had happened to pass even one Post Office in those two days, I might have leaped off the carriage, flipped Ben the bird (and I do not mean his Precious turkey), and looked for a sufficiently large Box. I was done with him and done messing around with the past, and as for the whole question of whether the future was still the same or screwed up and different from my Meddling, my answer was leaning heavily toward Let's Find Out.

But as you will See, all that changed once we got to

Philadelphia. One fact about the Days of Yore is that news travels a lot more slowly. In 2015, if an event of great importance takes place in Los Angeles, such as Justin Bieber getting a haircut, it will be heard about in New York one nanosecond later because of Technology. But in 1776, first of all Los Angeles didn't exist (in your *face*, Lakers fans!), and second of all the speed of communication is basically limited to how fast a horse can run or how far you can throw a newspaper. And since all the people we had encountered in the last ten days had basically been farmers who didn't leave their farms or coal miners who spent most of their waking hours underground, we had no idea 1) what to expect back in the City of Brotherly Love, 2) how long ago the Declaration of Independence and the Insane Map Those Jerks Made Up had reached King George or his Colonial Governors, or 3) what the British had decided to Do about it all.

It did not take us long to Ascertain some answers to these questions. Although I do not mean Us, because Benjamin Franklin was hiding in the back of the buggy with a malodorous blanket over his head, in case the people of Philly still wanted to rip off his arms and use them to beat him to death. Therefore it was just Yours Truly who parked the horse a few blocks from BF's pile of charred house-rubble—not wanting to park it too close in case that should arouse Suspicion—and took to the streets on a fact-finding mission.

Playing Igbert Fibbelstream had made me excellent at talking to strangers, and so it was with Confidence that I approached a pair of dudes chatting on a corner, in front of a place called the Sated Philadelphian, Purveyor of Fine Suppers for Men Ladies and Children. I have no idea why the owner of this establishment felt it necessary to specify that his meals were for Men Ladies and Children, since that's basically everybody. Maybe he had another store where he sold Hats Suitable for Wearing on Monday Tuesday Wednesday Thursday Friday Saturday and Sunday.

In any case, I walked right up to the dudes and said, "Salutations, good sirs. What news have you, for a lad newly arrived to this fair city?" Which might sound like a gooberish way of talking, but that was the Colonial fashion, and not to brag, but I had it pretty much mastered. It was all I could do not to pry up a cobblestone from the street and try to sell it to them.

One of the dudes, who I will call Ridiculous J. Mustache, turned to me with a scowl.

"Begone from us, posthaste!" he commanded in a strangled-sounding voice, and made a shooing motion.

I cocked my head at him, scowled right back, and did not move. "Have I given offense?" I asked, looking down to see if maybe I had some horse poop on me or something. This was not the type of reception I was used to getting, except maybe back in junior high.

"The Whispering Tariff!" said the other one, who I'll call Noseface, in a kind of agitated hiss.

"The what?"

"Have you not heard of the Whispering Tariff?" asked Ridiculous J. Mustache, obviously shocked. He took a giant step away from me, and then said, "It is a tax imposed when any more than two colonists congregate in public! And you are putting us all at risk!"

"So it's illegal for three people to have a conversation?" I said, totally perplexed.

Noseface nodded. "To prevent us from planning an uprising," he explained. "Three is considered a mob. Now move along before the redcoats see us. They are everywhere, and all the time!"

He glanced to his left, and I looked where he was

looking. Sure enough, four soldiers in red coats were marching toward us, with muskets at their sides. I scurried away from Noseface and Ridiculous J. Mustache, and busied myself pretending to read the menu of the restaurant.

"Where did they all come from?" I hissed at Ridiculous J. Mustache and Noseface once the soldiers had passed.

"King George has sent garrisons from New Jersey. We Philadelphians are seen as the most apt to rebel, since it was here that the Committee of Five met—a thousand curses on their names!" Ridiculous J. Mustache answered, seeming slightly more relaxed now that the patrol had passed. "I hear that Boston has also been swamped with them. And more are on the way, from the Empire's lands in the Caribbean and perhaps England as well."

"That sucks," I said, forgetting for a second what century I was in. But Ridiculous J. Mustache did not seem Perturbed by the word. He removed a pocket watch from his pants, and his eyes widened.

"It is five minutes to four!" he said in a tone of Alarm.

"It cannot be!" said Noseface, equally freaked out.

"So what?" I said. "What happens at four?"

"The Tea Law!" Noseface and Ridiculous J. Mustache said together.

"Tea is against the law?"

"Quite the contrary," said Noseface. "High tea is now mandatory. Failure to attend high tea promptly at four o'clock is viewed as sedition against the crown, and punishable by a public flogging in the town square!"

I thought for a moment. "Are we at least allowed to congregate for public floggings? Or do we have to show up two at a time?"

Noseface and Ridiculous J. Mustache looked at each other.

"That is a fine question," said Noseface. He pointed a spindly finger at me. "Now find yourself some tea," he said, before they both dashed off.

"And a crumpet!" added Ridiculous J. Mustache as he turned the corner and disappeared.

I stood there, dazed and flustered, and watched them go. The street, which had been bustling, was suddenly deserted.

It was only then that I noticed the poster affixed to the lamppost they had been standing before. On it were five Likenesses. BF, Jefferson, Adams, Sherman, and Livingston. Underneath were the words THE COMMITTEE OF FIVE: WANTED DEAD OR ALIVE. Someone had drawn a mustache on Jefferson, and a pair of pointy horns on BF.

I thought of him all alone, curled up beneath that stinky blanket in the back of the buggy, wanted dead or alive as his dreams of liberty burned down just like his house.

I forgive you, B-Freezy, I thought to myself. And weirdly, me forgiving him felt almost exactly the same as if he had forgiven me.

I ran back to the buggy at top speed, and climbed inside. The sound of snoring Emanated from beneath the blanket. I poked it, and the snoring stopped and BF grumbled and scrabbled at the blanket until his head was visible. He squinted at me, and something like a snarl happened with his mouth.

"*Now* you speak to me?" he grumbled. "What do you want?"

"The same thing you do," I said. "We don't have time to argue, BF. There's a Whispering Tariff and we'll get flogged if we don't drink tea, and I don't want to live in a future where this is the past. So whether you like it or not, I'm staying with you to save the country we love. We gotta do something and do it fast, only you can't be seen because you're wanted dead or alive and somebody drew horns on you."

It was a lot of information for somebody who had just

woken up. BF lifted his hand to his noggin. "While I was asleep? What scofflaw would do such a thing?"

"Not on you, on your poster. It's a bad scene, BF. There are British troops all over, and more coming, and everybody has to eat crumpets every day at four."

"I rather enjoy crumpets," said Ben, and yawned. Then he frowned. "I've just remembered that *I'm* not speaking to *you*."

"There's no time for pettiness, BF. The war is as good as lost unless we let bygones be bygones and be friends again so we can—"

Just then I glimpsed a flash of red out of the corner of my eye, and dove on top of Ben. "Stay down!" I whispered. "We're in violation of the Tea Law!" I could feel B-Freezy's chest heaving up and down beneath me, and then his hot breath in my ear.

"We must put aside our differences, young Franklin."

"I just said that, old Franklin. I literally *just* said that."

"Well, it bears repeating."

Ben sat up suddenly, causing me to slide off of his Considerable belly and onto the floor of the buggy in a heap of arms and legs.

"Ouch."

Ben looked over both shoulders. "Those red-clad representatives of the monarchy have passed out of sight." He offered me a hand. I took it, and he pulled me up and looked me in the eye.

"I withdraw my previous insults," he said. "They were made with a hot head and a cold heart, and do not reflect my deepest convictions regarding our relations."

"Was that like an apology?" I asked.

"It was not *like* an apology, you dunderheaded miscreant. It *was* an apology."

"You could just say 'sorry,'" I suggested. "Also, typically in an apology you don't insult the person further."

"'Sorry' is not a sentence, and furthermore it implies not an emotional state but a . . ."

Ben kept talking, but I stopped listening, because all this talk of apologies had reminded me of something, and that something was Claire Wanzandae, to whom I had made the major apology of my life so far.

More specifically, it reminded me that we were a few blocks away from B-Freezy's mailbox, assuming it was still standing, and that inside might Await a letter from two hundred and thirty-nine years in the future, written by a girl whose hair always smelled like cherry blossoms and gasoline.

A girl who hopefully had some kind of advice for us about how to save the day, and every day after the day. Because my own personal brain was not exactly overbrimming with super-excellent ideas.

CHAPTER 14

Dear Ike,

I don't think I slept more than a couple of hours a night between the time I sent my last letter and the day that I received yours back. I kissed it, if you want to know the truth, and also cried a couple of tears, like some lamebrained tragic girly-girl in a bad movie, which is totally not who I am. I ended up getting an A on that history midterm, for example, which proves that even when I am upset and fearing the worst, I still rock harder than sedimentary. That's a little Earth Science humor for you. Speaking of which, since you went "missing" I've been without a lab partner, which is a total drag. Nobody rock-catalogs like you, Ike.

Unfortunately, I cried *before* I kissed the letter, so when

I did kiss it I got ink all over my lips, and not just regular ink but whatever super-thick and extra-potent Colonial Blend you used, and then I couldn't get the ink off my lips. I had to cover it up by putting on some black lipstick I had left over from last Halloween, and go back to school like that (I have been coming home during lunch to check the mail), and now everybody thinks I'm some kind of Goth Girl, and this one Goth Dude named Garth (yup, Goth Garth) who I never even saw before asked me out on a date to see some band I never heard of called Plaguetacular or Plaguerific or something. Don't worry—I said no. But it's amazing what a little black lipstick can do.

What it cannot do though, Ike, is turn your disappearance into anything but an utter disaster for everyone concerned. And I do mean concerned. Your mother is still freaking out, and now everybody at school knows about your note too, because when she couldn't get any information from me or Ryan Demphill, your mother did everything you told her not to. She went to the cops and the newspaper, and told them both that you were missing and a runaway, and the next morning your photo and the letter were both on the eighth page of the *Philadelphia Gazette*. So things have gotten kind of hysterical around here. Everybody at school is speculating about where you went, with a weird mixture of respect and scorn and fear and wonder, plus a million other things swirled together. Basically, no one can imagine doing what they think you did, which is just say "screw it, I need a break from my life" and take off. To the average kid, that is totally inconceivable—although of course it is about one one-millionth as inconceivable as traveling backward in time to save the country from the ravages wrought upon it by a messy Claireike. So basically, Ike, you have become a legend.

But don't let that go to your head, because you know what else is inconceivable? The amount of stress and pain you are causing your poor mom. You really should have been more thoughtful about the impact this was going to have on her, although I admit that I don't know what you could have done differently. But before I go on in this letter, and tell you what has ME scared and what I think you should do about it, let me implore you, Ike: Stop whatever you are doing right now and write a letter to your mother and send it to me and I will make sure it gets to her—without the old-timey stamp, of course. They will want to see the postmark, but I will pretend to be stupid and say duh, I threw out the envelope, why, can you use a postmark to see where a letter comes from? They'll believe me, too, because nobody ever thinks kids know anything about anything.

Make up something that will ease her mind, Ike. Because it would be cruel not to, and the reassuring note you left does not prove to her that you are still okay ten days later. For all she knows you strolled out of the house and were immediately kidnapped or eaten by trolls or something. I mean, try to put yourself in her shoes. Imagine that you and I have kids someday, and that one day out of the blue one of those kids (let's say the boy, Hunter, assuming we have two girls and a boy and the girls are named Macalister and Tetragammon) just disappears and you don't see him for TEN DAYS. Would you take any comfort in the stupid little note he left before he VANISHED OFF THE FACE OF THE PLANET? I know I would take zero-point-zero-zero comfort in that, and if you are any kind of father, neither would you.

I know you have probably been too busy staying alive by wits alone to think about this stuff. That's understandable. I do not think you are a jerk or anything. But please, invent the most soothing story you can, write it down, and send it to me. I would tell you to stop reading right now and do that but a) I know you won't, and b) the rest of what I have to say is also of crucial importance. So here it is: my new theory about the past and how messing with it works.

I still think that whatever changes we have made to it haven't reached the point of unfixability, when they start to ripple forward and overwrite the future. Ben Franklin is still a hero according to Wikipedia, not some guy who destroyed our shot at independence and invented the Claireike (also, the Claireike still is not a thing, and if that ends up being the price we pay for continuing to exist, then I am cool with that).

But I am also pretty sure that we are quickly running out of time, because numerous historic milestones are coming, such as Colonial victories in various battles, and at some point I cannot help but believe that everything is going to collapse and the world I know is going be swallowed up into the black hole of the New World, which is so scary I cannot stop thinking about it. Maybe in the New World I don't even exist, Ike. Maybe there are no labradoodles. Or maybe a nuclear war destroyed us all in 1982 or something. Anything is possible. People say that a lot, "anything is possible," but I mean that LITERALLY ANYTHING is possible. The dodo bird might not have gone extinct in the 1790s. Maybe the world is overrun with dodo birds. Maybe a dodo bird killed John Lennon when he was an infant and the Beatles never existed. Maybe a talking bottle of ketchup is president of the United States. A girl can lose her mind, worrying about all the possibilities. I have to force myself to watch cartoons until I fall asleep, just to distract myself from it all. Cartoons are way better now than when we were little kids.

I have been researching my butt off, and talking to Mr. Larrapin so much that he probably thinks I'm a total nutcase, in order to provide you with some wise counsel about what to do next. By next I mean Before It Is Too Late, and by that I basically mean Right Now Now Now.

So here is what I have concluded: France. At this point, France is your only hope. According to Mr. Larrapin, the Colonies never would have won without France anyway. He says the American Revolution was pretty much a proxy war between the two main European powers, France and England, like when you don't invite a girl to your sleepover because you're mad that her best friend got chosen over you to give the closing argument on Debate Team. Except with ships and cannons and death. France put us over the top, but now that the British are really, really trying to win instead of being all "eh, whatever, we don't really care" about it, the ships and troops France eventually kicked in are not going to cut it, and we can't wait for that anyway because if we do the war will be over before it even starts.

BENJAMIN FRANKLIN

So the thing you and BF have absolutely, positively got to do is convince King Louis XVI of France to go all in, which luckily for you seems like the job B-Freezy was born to do. According to Mr. Larrapin, the French love him for some reason, the way German people love David Hasselhoff. And right now, Louis XVI is probably sitting at his summer palace in Versailles, wondering whether to go all in or not. He and King George are basically two guys playing poker, and KG has just pushed all his chips into the middle of the table and KL has to decide whether to fold or call. Do you play poker? I don't think we ever discussed it. My family plays every Sunday night. I'm really good.

So anyway, that's what I've got. I wish I could be more helpful in terms of helping you figure out how to get to France and score an audience with the king, but I'm sure you and Ben can figure that part out. Versailles is supposed to be beautiful, with the best gardens anybody has ever planted in the history of the world. Check it out really carefully, so you can tell me all about it when you COME HOME. You should do that SOON. Before I start dating GOTH GARTH. Just kidding. But seriously. Fix the past and get back here, because I miss you. But before you do that, write a letter to your mother. Make up something that sounds really, really safe.

Kisses to you, Ike. And a hug for Ben. I feel like I know him, you know what I mean? How weird is that?

I am,
Claire Wanzandae

CHAPTER 15

It was not difficult to convince B-Freezy that Claire Wanzandae was right, and we had to go to France. It turned out he had been thinking along similar Lines.

"It is the conclusion that any sensible man of Politics would reach," he said gravely. We were sitting in the back of the buggy, which was sitting in an alley. I didn't know how long High Tea was supposed to last, but I figured the smart thing to do was stay off the streets until they were no longer deserted. There was also the fact that BF couldn't be seen even when it wasn't tea time—not without a much better disguise than Bald 'n' Bearded, like maybe a bear suit.

"Today is Wednesday, is it not?" he asked.

"If you say so. I've pretty much lost track."

"There is a ship leaving tonight, for the port of France. How much money do we have?"

"Let me check." I pulled a wad of bills from my pocket and started to organize them by denomination. I could feel B-Freezy's impatience, which for some reason made me want to count even slower. I guess I wasn't one hundred percent done being mad at him for being mad at me. Maybe like 94 percent.

"Two hundred and six bucks," I said at last. "Will that buy us two tickets to frog country, or what?"

Ben's face grew dark beneath the scruffy beard that made him look like a very old terrier with a skin condition. "I daresay it will not," he muttered. "The cost of a transatlantic voyage is a hundred and twenty-five dollars per person, in a shared stateroom . . . in *steerage*." He shuddered. "I never dreamed that I, Benjamin Franklin, Founding Father, states-man, inventor, printer, author, politician, scientist, musician, philosopher, and creator of the postal system, would lack the funds to travel in steerage. So named, presumably, because it is barely fit for cattle."

"Beggars can't be choosers, BF. You can have that expres-sion if you want."

He snorted. "You would have to travel backward through time an additional two hundred years in order to claim authorship of that phrase. Now. Let us turn to more practical matters. We need an additional forty-four dollars, and we have but ninety minutes to reach the harbor and book our passage. Otherwise, we shall have to wait an additional week, and our country can scarce afford That."

I thought for a moment. And then it hit me like a satchel full of bricks, and I climbed into the front of the buggy and grabbed the reins.

"Take us to Thirty-Three Lancaster Avenue!" I ordered Lambo. He responded by attempting to bite a fly that had settled on his left rear flank. I turned to Ben.

"Take us to Thirty-Three Lancaster Avenue!" I said.

"Make a right at the end of this alley, and then your second left," BF instructed. And then, "What awaits us at Thirty-Three Lancaster Avenue?"

"Help," I said, crossing my fingers that it was true.

* * *

"Wait here," I told Ben, five minutes later, as we arrived at the address. I leaped down from the buggy, rubbed Lambo on the muzzle, and opened the white gate that stood before the large white house. I marched up the walkway, seized hold of the brass knocker, and thumped it hard against the door.

I heard footsteps from within the house, and then the door swung open.

Before me stood the Young Scamp. In his hand was a turkey drumstick bigger than his forearm, and on his face was an Abundance of turkey grease, which he presently wiped off with the sleeve of his white shirt, turning it translucent.

"What do *you* want?" he asked, and gnawed a sliver of meat from the drumstick.

"A ride to the harbor," I said.

He snorted at me. "That is perfectly legal, and therefore of no interest to me."

"It is not legal in the least," I assured him. "You will be transporting illegal cargo, helping a fugitive flee the country, and taking delivery of stolen merchandise."

The Young Scamp considered this. "Better," he said, and tossed the turkey bone carelessly onto his own front lawn, which was basically a stinking Graveyard of food-related trash. "What is the cargo?"

"The cargo is the fugitive." I turned and pointed at our

Vehicle. "How much would you say that buggy is worth?"

The Young Scamp gave it a look of Sizing-up. "Fifty dollars," he said.

"The horse and buggy together," I said, wanting to Clarify.

"Fifty-five."

"They are both yours in return for forty-four dollars and a ride to the harbor."

"And they are stolen?"

"Not only are they stolen, but they have been the means of transport for an elaborate criminal enterprise that has swindled and deceived hundreds of people," I told him, feeling myself morph into Igbert Fibbelstream. "And the horse is also a murderer. He has trampled three men to death at our command."

That was totally nonsense, but it seemed to impress the Young Scamp. "You've got yourself a deal," he said, and we shook hands. His, unsurprisingly, was very greasy.

"Good," I said. "And one more thing. Do you have some kind of garment that our fugitive could wear, to disguise himself?"

"This is not a costume shoppe," the Young Scamp informed me. "But I am the best driver in all of Philadelphia, and I will deliver you directly to your ship without Benjamin Franklin being seen."

"How did you know it was Benjamin Franklin?" I asked.

"Because I am not an idiot," the Young Scamp answered.

In less than a minute's Time, Lamborghini was flying through the streets at a pace that was remarkable to me.

"How do you make him run so fast?" I called from the backseat. "I could barely make him trot."

"I already told you," the Young Scamp called back, taking a large bite from yet another turkey leg. Apparently, his home contained nothing but Recently Cooked Fowl. "I am the best driver in the city. Now cease distracting me." He took another mouthful from his turkey leg, then placed it on the seat beside him and dropped the reins, in order to lift a gallon jug of lemonade to his lips and take a giant swig.

In what seemed like no time at all, we had reached the harbor. There were about twenty piers with ships large and small docked at them, but it was obvious right away which one was ours—it was enormous, and all kinds of people with steamer trunks and giant suitcases were standing around in front of it, boarding and waiting to board. There were a bunch of sailors or porters or something, loading stuff onto the ship, and a guy in some kind of fancy-pants pants and a frilly frock-coat who seemed to be taking money and giving out tickets or receipts.

"Rats fleeing a sinking ship," muttered B-Freezy, peering out at the scene.

"They're getting *on* the ship," I pointed out, then realized that he meant the sinking ship was America.

"I cannot get you any closer," said the Young Scamp, bringing the horse to a Halt. "From here, you must walk." We climbed out of the buggy, BF wrapping the filthy blanket around his back like a shawl. The Young Scamp took a wad of money out of his pocket, and handed it over. "Forty-four dollars," he said. And with that, he was gone.

"Hide," Ben suddenly said in a fierce whisper, pulling the blanket over his head and walking swiftly, for him, in the wrong direction.

"What—" I started to say, but then I looked behind BF and saw what he had seen, or rather Whom.

Josiah the Jerk was walking down the pier, his cutlass swinging by his side and a jug in his hand. My guess was, it contained something stronger than unsweetened lemonade.

I couldn't move. I just stood there, frozen, looking up at him like some kind of Moronic Sunflower as he drew closer and closer. And then he was standing right before me, scowling the scowliest scowl I had ever seen in my short and possibly about-to-end life.

"What're ye lookin' at?" he growled. "Outta my way, ya wee—"

Then he looked closer. "Well! Pickle my tongue. If it ain't the young scoundrel what helped the old scoundrel escape me inn." He grabbed me by the shoulder and bent low at the waist, until we were eye-to-eye. "I'll cut out yer liver and feed it ta me house cat," he said.

"Help!" I cried—or tried to, but Josiah the Jerk clamped a hand over my mouth. A hand that smelled like smoked fish and booze.

"Shush, shush. There's no point in exertin' yerself, ya scalawag. Yer as good as gutted already."

I looked around frantically, searching for Ben. But he was nowhere to be seen. Josiah drew his cutlass, and lifted it slowly toward my neck.

"Ye should not have crossed a man like me," he said, and grinned a sicko grin. I closed my eyes and waited for the end to come. My whole life flashed before me—throwing rocks at hornets' nests with Ryan Demphill in kindergarten, my mom and dad sitting me down to tell me Dad was moving out, the night Mom came back from the hospital with baby

Carolyn and she clamped her tiny little hand around my pinky finger, and then a series of more recent stuff like kissing Claire Wanzandae, throwing up on Claire Wanzandae, taping myself into a box, and shaving Ben Franklin's head.

All at once, as I waited for Josiah the Jerk's cutlass to slice a vent into my throat, I knew what was important like never before. Fixing my mistakes and saving my country were fine and noble and all that, but really, the most important thing was being with the people you loved. I should have been back home, with my mom and Caro and Claire Wanzandae, and if I lived through the next thirty seconds, which seemed highly unlikely, I was going to get my butt back to 2015 as soon as was humanly possible.

And if I died, maybe I could still be born in 2002.

I squeezed my eyes tighter, and wondered what was taking so long.

Then I heard a dull thwacking sound, and opened my eyes in time to see Josiah the Jerk's eyes roll back in his head. He fell to the ground before me, the cutlass clattering across the pier and then kerplunking into the water. Behind him stood B-Freezy, a wooden plank in his hand.

"That concludes that conversation," he said. "Come on now, sonny boy."

I stepped across the unconscious body of Josiah the Jerk, and together Ben and I walked swiftly toward the ship. My heart was still pounding in my chest, partly from residual fear and partly from a weird Joy at being alive and also at being called "sonny boy" by BF because that sounded not just friendly but downright Affectionate, like something your grandfather would call you.

Ben gave my arm a squeeze, and winked at me. "Buy passage," he whispered. "Do not give our real names to the purser, but instead make something up. I shall wait here, and attempt to be Inconspicuous."

"Roger that," I said.

"Roger That seems a poor alias," Ben replied.

"No, I didn't— Never mind. I'll be right back."

A moment later, I was handing two hundred and fifty dollars over to the fancy-pants guy, the purser or whatever. He counted it out even slower than I had, deposited the money in a giant purse-type thing that was practically over-flowing with cash, and wrote me out an elaborate receipt in fancy-pants handwriting.

"Your names?" he asked.

"Count Dracula and Luke Skywalker," I said.

Fancy-pants raised an eyebrow. "A count?"

"Yeah," I said. "He's from Transylvania. I'm his translator. I learned Transylvanian from my family's butler, when I was a lad."

One thing I had learned as Igbert Fibbelstream, and also before that as Lying Ike, was that if you're going to lie, go big. If you stay close to the truth, you are liable to confuse yourself, or box yourself in. Whereas if you journey a good distance Away from it, you have room to stretch out your wings and improvise.

The purser raised his eyebrow at me for a moment, and I felt my butt clench up. Then he looked back down at his Ship's Manifesto, and said in a bored voice, "The Count's Christian name?" and I relaxed.

"Vladimir," I told him.

"Enjoy your voyage," the purser said. "These men will convey your luggage to your stateroom."

"Very good," I said, declining to mention that we Had none. "And may I leave a letter in your care, before we commence our voyage?"

"Certainly," he said. "Have you the letter now, or do you intend to compose it in the thirty minutes before the ship pushes off?"

"I will compose it now."

"Very good," the purser said, with a curt nod.

The next thing I knew, the Count and I were boarding the ship. I ran ahead to our stateroom, wrote my mother the most comforting letter I could, finished with five minutes to spare, and ran it down to the purser. Until I could do my duty to my country, save the future, and return to my own Time in glory, some well-chosen Words would have to Suffice.

CHAPTER 16

Dear Mom,

I am writing you this letter to say: All is well and I am safe and sound. I know you probably will not relax until I am back at home under your watchful eyes, and also grounded until Alien Overlords rule the earth, which is fine and probably what I deserve. But hopefully you can take some solace in Knowing that I am not in any danger whatsoever, or caught up in any type of weird or unsavory situation. I am just taking a break to clear my head, like I said in my Note. I am also very, very, very extremely sorry to have caused you so much worry. It was selfish of me, I know. But sometimes a guy just has to get away from it all and reboot his hard drive, and this is one of those times. By hard drive, I mean Brain.

You've Got Mail

I am sure some specific Information would be helpful, so I will tell you as much as I can without being so detailed that you or the police or anybody will come and get me before I am ready to return. I am at a Yoga Retreat in a remote location, very far or maybe not so far from Philadelphia, at a place that does not have a website and is completely off the grid. I found it through word of mouth among the Yoga Community, and got a Scholarship to come. Also, they don't believe in ballpoint pens, which is why I am writing this letter with a Quill and an inkwell. Please ignore the smudges.

You may be surprised to know that I am a part of the Yoga Community, but I have been quietly practicing Yoga for many months now, only I kept it to myself because I just felt like it, and also Dirk would have made fun of me because as you know he is basically a Cro-Magnon Man. I would also like to take this opportunity to point out that I probably would not need this Break from my life if Dirk was not such a big part of it, because living with that dude is like a constant punishment due to his various obnoxious habits and his Attitude toward me. I am sorry to Diss your husband and the father of my awesome sister like that, but frankly I do not think you are all that wildly happy being married to Dirk either, since the two of you bicker basically all the time, and besides I might as well be honest in this letter since Yoga is all about finding your true Inner Self and also I don't think my feelings about Dirk are all that surprising anyway. Maybe seeing these Facts about him written out in Old-Timey ink will make you take them more seriously, though I will not hold my breath. Especially since Yoga is all about breathing.

Anyway, like I was saying, I am actually a Second Degree Black Belt in Yoga, but part of my Technique is that I only do my yoga in private because actually it is a top secret type of yoga that was invented by a Shaolin Monk and is only taught to students of exceptional promise, like me. I should not even be telling you this, Mom. But anyway, please do not ever ask me to Demonstrate this yoga, because if I show it to outsiders I could be Assassinated by the secret Yoga Ninja Squad that lives here and does all the cooking and yard work.

That is pretty much the Gist of it. Every morning, I wake up after a restful sleep and eat a light but delicious breakfast of miso soup and Tandoori Chicken, which is left outside the paper sliding doors of my bungalow by the Ninjas. Then I meditate for a few hours, eat the lunch that is left outside my door, usually some kind of vegetable curry featuring produce from the Yoga Center's organic garden. Then I practice my yoga until dinnertime. We all eat dinner together, and after dinner there are lectures by different famous yoga masters. Famous within the Yoga Community, I mean. You would not have heard of them.

I am the second-youngest person here, after a seven-year-old yoga prodigy from Transylvania, so everybody goes out of their way to take excellent care of me. We are like one big family, Mom. A family with no wisecracking stepfathers who make fun of everything. I can feel my head clearing, and my Energy becoming focused, and my body growing strong and supple. Some of the instructors here have even started calling me The One and whispering that I may be the fulfillment of an ancient prophecy. I will come back soon, very soon, and until I do please rest Assured that I am not only safe but happy and in good Hands.

Give Caro a big hug and kiss for me. And give yourself one of Each also. I will see you both soon.

Your Loving and Apologetic Son,
Ike

CHAPTER 17

From the Journal of Benjamin Franklin

At this juncture I must address a query that I am certain even the most casual reader is posing: whether wet ink is dripping onto my face as I write in this journal, lying on my back in a hammock that is swaying in concert with the motion of this vessel. The answer is a most emphatic "Yes." As I scribe these very words, my countenance sports a series of black splotches, making me look more like a Bubonic Plague patient than a Founding Father, statesman, inventor, printer, author, politician, scientist, musician, philosopher, and venerable creator of the very postal system that begat my fugitive traveler and my current situation.

Still, after due consideration, I have concluded that this network of canvas webs is superior to the bunk beds available in the more expensive rooms of this ship. Mainly because the sides wrap around the sleeper like a cocoon, making it virtually impossible to fall. This is more vital than comfort, as Ike is occupying the berth above me and the notion of him falling on top of me during swells or rough seas is troublesome enough that it would prevent me from ever falling asleep during this six-week crossing of the Atlantic.

"Psst. B-Freezy. Are you asleep?"

My initial instinct was to pretend I was, thus ridding me of the obligation of participating in a conversation that promised to be, at very best, inane. It was the first evening of our first day aboard the *Breakwind* and I was suffering the disorientation that comes from lying on one's back in the dark and speaking upward toward someone whose bony posterior droops mere inches above your ink-stained face.

Yet, there was something in his tone that gave me pause. It seemed tinged with longing. As if to deny it would confirm the insecurity from whence it emerged. Therefore, because I am a man of compassion, I lowered any standard I held for stimulating discourse and opted to answer.

"I am not," I admitted.

"I was just wondering," Ike said, his voice quavering like my neck does on a windy day, "whether you and me are friends." His speech became rapid, the words tumbling over one another as they cascaded from his mouth. "I mean, you know, you called me 'Sonny Boy' back on the docks after you hit Josiah with that plank, and something about that felt really good. So I was wondering if we were friends now, or even family. Or not."

I must confess that I was touched by Ike's clumsy outpouring of sentiment.

I was about to respond that we were indeed friends, and that if an imagined familial bond was a thing of comfort to him then I had no objection to maintaining it. But at that moment, our mutual attention was diverted by loud thumping sounds overhead, followed by laughter.

"Do you hear that, B-Freezy?"

"I am not deaf."

Another thump resounded through our chamber, and then another laugh.

"It sounds like it's coming from the deck above us," said Ike. "Then again, all of the decks are above us." He turned in his hammock and peered down me.

"Let us seek out the source of this thumping and laughing," I proposed, as a fourth thump and then a fourth laugh shook our humble stateroom.

"Word," Ike answered, like a person who, instead of a brain, has a bin full of words written on slips of paper, and whose method of communication is to select and speak them at random with no regard to their meaning.

"Rotunda," I answered, to prove that I, too, could play That game. And with no more conversation between us, we climbed to the foredeck.

* * *

We arrived in the ship's main drawing room to find a gathering of seated passengers, dressed as if for the theater. On the stage before them were two circus clowns with thick makeup and autumnal-colored hair, holding

129

what appeared to be large rubber mallets. Theirs was a performance seemingly conceived for an audience of mentally deficient schoolchildren. It consisted entirely of the taller, thinner clown asking the shorter, portlier one a series of questions. If the responses were incorrect, he then struck the shorter clown in his ample paunch with the mallet, toppling him onto his posterior.

"Do tell, what level of this sailing vessel possesses the foulest odor?" asked the taller clown.

"The poop deck?" responded the shorter, stouter clown, whereupon the audience howled. They exuded even greater gales of merriment when the taller clown punctuated his disapproval by administering blunt force to the shorter clown's stomach with the aforementioned mallet.

"I didn't know poop jokes were this old," Ike whispered, after he, too, had ceased his uproarious guffaws.

"Nor did I," I said grimly, for I saw little Humor in the rank doings of these two makeup-covered buffoons.

"Lighten up, B-Freezy. A good poop joke is a thing of beauty."

I did not bother to respond, but turned my attention back to the disgusting duo before me, in time to see the portly clown regain his feet and dust off his gargantuan backside.

"Do tell," queried the taller clown, "why is pirating so addictive?"

"Because," rejoined the stouter, "once you lose your first hand, you become hooked!"

Again, the mallet knocked him to the ground and the crowd roared. As he began to right himself, I took note of the upward curl of his lip. It was familiar to me. And despite the stage makeup, so was the downward arc of his right eyebrow. I had seen it before. On innumerable occasions. Whenever John Adams of Massachusetts was considering a proposal during our meetings of the Committee of Five.

I turned again to the rambunctious imbeciles onstage, watching them with a keener eye. Was it possible that this was indeed John Adams of Massachusetts who stood before me, masquerading as a common clown?

It was no less possible, I concluded, than the fact that the author, inventor, diplomat, scientist, printer, statesman, and Founding Father who stood watching him was listed on the ship's manifest as Count Vladimir Dracula of Transylvania.

"I pray thee," intoned the clown of greater height, "why do young pirates always fail when reciting the alphabet?"

"Because their fathers insist that there are seven Cs!" rejoined the shorter, and when he again fell victim to the mallet, I could barely restrain myself from exclaiming *quod erat demonstrandum*, or "it is demonstrated" in the Latin, for now I espied not only the telltale upturned lip and downward-arcing brow of John Adams of Massachusetts upon the visage of the diminutive clown, but also a familiar haughty sneer of discontent upon the visage of the taller.

I knew it all too well. It was perfectly reminiscent of the look that Thomas Jefferson of Virginia had cast my way on the afternoon of a recent thunderstorm, when I requested to borrow one of the two umbrellas he had brought.

"Do you not possess an umbrella of your own, Benjamin Franklin of Philadelphia?" he had asked.

"I do, but this morning's sky bore no suggestion

of this downpour," I had explained. "Now, may I borrow one? For I feel the onset of a cold, and I fear that unshielded exposure to this storm may graduate it to a more grave medical condition, such as a bad cold."

"I am not predisposed to making such a loan, out of concern for my own health."

"But you have two umbrellas!"

"At this moment, yes. But should a strong wind happen to turn my umbrella inside out, it would be I who was in danger of contracting a fatal disease. That is the reason I carry two, even on balmy days, with respect to the capriciousness of cloud movement," he said, flashing a haughty sneer of discontent and poking me in the ribs with one of the umbrellas, and then, after a short pause, the other.

"Come, sonny boy," I said to Ike, as a way of answering his still-unanswered question regarding our friendship.

"But this is really funny! Besides, there's nothing else to do," he whined.

"Do not talk back to Count Dracula," I said. And seizing him by the ear, I dragged him belowdecks.

"What's your problem, dude?" he asked me in a high-pitched tone, as we stood before an endless bank of staterooms far more luxurious than our own.

"Those buffoons were not the buffoons they purport to be," I announced. "They, like we, are in disguise."

"Of course they are. Nobody has a nose that red in real life, except maybe you."

I cuffed him lightly on the head, to refocus his attention.

"Ow. What the heck is wrong with you?"

"Those clowns were John Adams of Massachusetts and Thomas Jefferson of Virginia," I told him. "And I intend to locate their staterooms and lie in wait for them. And perhaps eat any snacks they might have chanced to leave behind for later."

No sooner had I said it than, with a clamor of clown feet upon metal, those selfsame Founding Fathers shuffled down the staircase and stood before us. The sneer of haughty discontent was gone now, as were the curled lip and the down-arcing eyebrow. Instead, upon their faces were matching expressions of astonishment, and even, dare I say, joy.

"It cannot be," whispered Thomas Jefferson of

Virginia, with characteristic incorrectness. "Benjamin Franklin of Philadelphia? Thank Providence! We had given you up for dead!"

"And yet it is," murmured John Adams of Massachusetts, with characteristic stating of the obvious, and he reached out to touch my face.

I slapped his hand away as if it were an errant mosquito, and said, "You two are quite the pair of clowns."

Jefferson and Adams bowed deeply.

"Thank you," they said in unison.

CHAPTER 18

So there we were, in T-Jeff and Johnny Adrock's stateroom. To be honest, I didn't know what to expect. After all the stories and complaints I'd heard from B-Freezy, I wasn't sure if these dudes were his friends or his enemies. Or maybe his frenemies, although I was pretty sure that term and possibly that Concept did not yet exist. I made a mental note to invent it.

Nobody was saying anything, so I figured I'd break the ice by encouraging Ben to not be a jerk, despite his Tendency to be a jerk.

"Hey, Ben," I said, smiling nice and wide, "you must also be relieved to see your old buddies here alive and well, huh?"

He made a snorty little sound, like a horse who has been disrespected, and said, "Some believe that when a man abandons his dignity, he is already dead."

T-Jeff and Johnny Adrock didn't like that one bit.

"And some believe that a man who has caused years of work to crumble into ruins for the sake of a delectable new Snack should not criticize others for what they have done to survive the havoc he has wrought!" T-Jeff thundered, coming so close to BF's face that the tips of their noses were almost touching.

"Nor should a man who has taken to tricking rural laborers into thinking the juice of the apple can cure all their ills give out insults!" added Johnny Adrock.

"Oh yes," said T-Jeff, nodding his head. "Word of your felonious exploits has reached us, Benjamin Franklin of Philadelphia—or should I say Dr. Hezekiah J. Fibbelstream of Nowhere?"

B-Freezy opened his mouth, but no words came out. Johnny Adrock started right back in again.

"And now, after scuttling our war effort with your foolish maps and your delicious Claireikes, I suppose you think you can save our fledgling country by crossing the Atlantic and pleading the Colonies' case to King Louis XVI of France, when that is rightfully our mission?"

"You're darn right he does!" I shouted, and all three of them gasped.

"There is no need for foul language," T-Jeff sputtered. "Who is this uncouth person? The young partner in your medical swindling business, I must assume."

"You assume right," I said, feeling the heat rise into my cheeks. "And don't you dare talk to the ambassador like that. He's put up with enough of your bullying, and he's not going to stand for it anymore, are you, B-Freezy?"

Johnny Adrock cackled. "Who in Providence is B-Freezy?"

"I am," said B-Freezy, straightening his back and looking them both right in the eye. "And my young friend Ike is right."

On "friend," he winked at me, as if to say *yes, we are friends.* I winked back, then listened as he resumed tearing Johnny Adrock and T-Jeff a pair of new buttholes.

"I have endured your insults and slights, your undelivered party invitations and un-lent umbrellas, for far too long. Perhaps the Claireike contributed to our current predicament, but without my Vision we would never have drafted a Declaration of Independence to begin with. I was writing, printing, inventing, and ambassadoring when both of you were still soiling your pants, and I have had Enough!"

And with that, B-Freezy slammed his fist against a

nearby nightstand, causing it to topple over onto the ground. "If you think I would allow two novice politicians like yourselves to plead our case before the French King, then you are sorely mistaken. I have more diplomatic skill in my smallest finger than either of you possess in your entire foolishly attired bodies!"

"How dare you insult me, B-Freezy of Philadelphia?" snapped T-Jeff. "It is I who wrote the Declaration of Independence, lest you forget."

"Only by dint of superior penmanship did you write the Declaration of Independence," Ben roared right back. "But it is just like you to claim credit for the thoughts you merely scribbled down!"

"Okay," I said, before anybody else could talk. "Enough bickering. You guys are worse than a bunch of thirteen-year-olds."

"How dare—" Johnny Adrock began, but I talked right over him. Like a BOSS.

"First of all, you worked on the Declapendence together, okay? Everybody contributed, so stop being catty about that, all of you."

"Declapendence?" repeated T-Jeff.

"Is that some sort of abbreviation? How dare you

abbreviate the greatest document in the history of human endeavor!" demanded Adams.

"I rather like Declapendence," said T-Jeff. "It has a lilting ring."

"Me too," said Adams, after a moment.

"I invented the term," said B-Freezy, and I decided to let him have that one.

"Second of all," I went on, "we're all in this together. We can spend the voyage arguing over who gets to talk to Louis XVI, or we can decide right now that we're going as a team, and start figuring out what the heck we're gonna say."

Nobody said anything. B-Freezy regarded them warily for a while. They regarded him back with an equal amount of wariness.

I waited.

Then I got sick of waiting.

"Stop regarding one another warily," I said. "It's boring and dumb. What do you guys care about, huh? Feuding with one another like a bunch of schoolchildren, or saving the country?"

"You speak incessantly for one so young," Johnny Adrock said, in a tone that was definitely Unkind.

"You speak incessantly for one so fat," I shot back.

Which wasn't really fair, since he wasn't all that fat. Though he could have stood to lose maybe twenty-five pounds. I made a mental note to invent Pilates.

Johnny Adrock's face grew redder and redder, and I began to tremble in fear.

Then he burst out laughing. T-Jeff and B-Freezy joined in, and so did I.

"This impudent rapscallion is correct," T-Jeff said at last. "You are fat, and we must put aside our grievances and collaborate on a proposal, lest King George and his army dash our hopes of independence once and for all."

"Agreed," said Johnny Adrock. "We must renew and honor our alliance, and I shall endeavor to consume fewer potpies."

"Forgive my insults, Thomas Jefferson of Virginia," said B-Freezy, offering his hand. Jefferson took it, and they shook.

"Forgive mine," he said. "I should have invited you to that party at my sister's house, and lent you that umbrella."

"Think nothing of it," BF said. He turned to shake hands with Adams, and then turned toward me. "Now. Let us thank my young friend—our young friend—Ike Saturday, for his words of wisdom." Next thing I knew, all three of them were lining up to shake hands with me. Jefferson's hand was bony. Adams's was sweaty. BF's was sandpapery and cool.

"Nobody has ever accused me of Possessing wisdom before, BF," I said as we shook.

"There is a first time for everything," Ben replied, and gave me another wink.

"Let us get down to business," said T-Jeff when we were done, pulling up chairs for us and seating himself on the edge of the bed. Their room really was a lot nicer than ours. "What proposal shall we bring to the court of the king, Ambassador Franklin?"

"Well," said Ben, spreading his hands, "our needs are manifold. We must request the intervention of his army. And as much money as possible, to outfit our own soldiers with munitions and the like."

"Indeed," said Johnny Adrock, as T-Jeff nodded. I wondered if either of them remembered that they were still wearing full clown makeup.

"That's the easy part," I said. "The real question is, what are we gonna offer him? It's gotta be an offer he can't refuse. And keep in mind he's already kicking back and relaxing in a super-beautiful garden, eating delicious French food, so we've really gotta knock his socks off."

"Who are you, anyway?" said Thomas Jefferson, "I mean no offense, but I for one would like to know from whence you came, and how you become part of this 'we,' which is otherwise composed of accomplished statesmen?"

"As would I," Adams concurred. "For had you been present before, we might have called our convening the Committee of Five and One Half."

"Ha-ha, John Adams of Massachusetts," I said. "You're about as funny as King George pooping all over the Declapendence."

"I concur that John Adams of Massachusetts is not funny," said T-Jeff. "But his question is a fair one. Who are you, young master, and why should we listen to your counsel?"

A feeling of Uh-Oh rolled around in my stomach. I looked over at BF. He gave me a tiny nod, so I said, "My name is Franklin Isaac Saturday, and you should listen to me because I traveled here from the year 2015."

"That is preposterous," said Johnny Adrock. Then he looked at B-Freezy and T-Jeff, and added, "Isn't it?"

"I thought so at first," BF said slowly. "But the evidence is incontrovertible. Observe."

He removed a crumpled piece of paper from his pocket,

and handed it to Adams. Adams unfolded it and furrowed his brow.

"This appears to be some form of currency, bearing your likeness upon it," he said. "And bearing the date 2006. How remarkable."

"That fateful map depicting all fifty United States of America is also from the future," B-Freezy added. "Freedom is our destiny. We are to be a nation of great size. Or, at least, it was so, before the future landed atop the past when this Lad took it upon himself to misuse the postal system I invented, and mail himself to our Time."

There was a long patch of silence as they took that information In. Then, at the exact same moment, T-Jeff and Johnny Adrock both said, "Is my likeness also on a form of currency?"

"You, yes. You, no."

Jefferson smiled. Adams poked out his lower lip and pouted.

"I suppose we know whom posterity holds to be the superior statesman," Jefferson crowed.

"Yeah," I said. "That would be B-Freezy. The hundred is the biggest bill there is, and we even call it a Benjamin.

You're on the nickel, Jefferson, which is basically worthless. People mostly throw them in fountains when they want to make a wish."

"Curses," muttered T-Jeff under his breath.

"If you are truly from the future," said Johnny Adrock, "then Providence has blessed us with a formidable weapon to deploy against the king's aggression. Imagine our fortune, to have benefit of more than two hundred years' worth of knowledge!"

"Were it only so," said B-Freezy. "He is a spirited lad, to be sure. And quite ingenious. But he is . . . How shall I say it? No great student of history."

The Committee of Three stared at me.

"I know a few things," I said. "After all, I invented the Claireike."

Johnny Adrock licked his lips. "Have you any Claireikes on your person now?"

"No."

"Then, in summary, you possess neither knowledge of the future nor snacks?"

"I've got boatloads of knowledge. If I wasn't so busy helping you guys save the country, I'd be getting rich inventing all kinds of stuff, from baseball to . . . uh . . . basketball. But what we need right now isn't knowledge, it's a plan."

"Let us offer King Louis XVI the exclusive right to sell wine in liberated America," said John Adams. "That way, we shall secure his help and also ensure that we have robust, hearty reds and sophisticated, effervescent whites with which to toast our victory."

"That is the stupidest idea I have ever heard in my life," I said.

"Have you some problem of a personal nature with me?" demanded Johnny Adrock.

"No. I just know a dumb idea when I hear one. Jeez," I said, shaking my head. "How did a clown like you ever become president?"

Adams's eyes lit up. "I am to be president?"

"Yeah, after Washington."

"George Washington? That self-mythologizing, childless braggart?"

"Uh-huh."

"Do I also become president?" asked B-Freezy and T-Jeff at the same time.

"You, no, you, yes."

"Hurrah," cheered Jefferson.

"I'd sooner hold an overbrimming spittoon than that position," declared Ben.

Jefferson cleared his throat. "Hate not the player, B-Freezy of Philadelphia, but rather hate the game."

"Uh, guys?" I said. "If we don't convince France to jump in, nobody's going to be president *or* hold an overbrimming spittoon."

"Agreed," said Adams. "Let us then make him, as you said, an offer he cannot refuse. All the land west of the Mississippi River."

"Verily, you are a maelstrom of badly conceived ideas," said B-Freezy.

"Indeed. If Master Ike's map is to be believed, that is two-thirds of our land!" said Jefferson. "We would be saving the nation only to hand it over to some frog-eating Frenchman!"

"California turns out to be pretty rad," I agreed. "First they're gonna find gold there, and then after that the Lakers are pretty dominant, with Magic and Kareem and then Shaq and Kobe."

"Is this Gang Up On John Adams of Massachusetts Day?" sputtered John Adams of Massachusetts. "For if so, I was not informed."

"If you had been informed, you would no doubt have made an asinine suggestion about that as well," T-Jeff replied.

"Founding Fathers, please," I said. "Shut your pieholes. I've got it."

To my Shock, they fell silent and waited.

"Florida," I said. "We offer him Florida."

"But Florida is enormous," protested Ben. "Not to mention, a British colony."

"Soon they're gonna sell it to Spain. But it doesn't matter. The point is, promise it to the French. Trust me, it's a win-win. They get a giant piece of land, and we get rid of Florida."

"What is the matter with Florida?"

"Everything. The swampy weather makes people go insane. Every time you hear a news story like 'Man running across freeway holding bucket of worms attacked by man running across freeway holding bucket of fishing rods' or 'Police officer found guilty of conspiring to cook and eat suspect in racketeering case,' it's in Florida. There's some okay beaches, and I've got nothing against retired people, but trust me, it's gonna be a total embarrassment to the country. We're better off without it."

Adams picked up the nightstand BF had knocked over, and slammed his fist against it. It fell over again.

"Florida must go!" he bellowed.

Jefferson picked up the nightstand and slammed his fist against it, toppling it once more.

"I concur!" he shouted.

I righted the nightstand, slammed my fist against it, and knocked it on its side. "What time is dinner?" I bellowed. "I'm starving!"

Ben retrieved the nightstand, and slammed his fist against it. "As am I!" he roared, as the nightstand fell onto its side.

"Why is everyone hitting this nightstand?" demanded Jefferson at the top of his lungs, picking up the nightstand and pounding it with his fist until it toppled sideways.

There were only five and a half weeks left until we reached France.

CHAPTER 19

Dear Claire Wanzandae,

You know how before you are supposed to stand up in front of the whole biology class and present your report on lemurs or whatever, you feel a kind of nervous Dread in your stomach, and you wish it was time to rock and roll already because actually Doing it is not so bad, but the anticipation of doing it makes you want to scream and yank out big fistfuls of your own hair and eat them with Bolognese sauce? That is basically how I have felt for the last five and a half weeks, waiting for the *Breakwind* to reach France.

Also, before I go any further, a brief note on the *Breakwind*. I did not think I possessed the maturity to Not make any jokes about being on a ship named after an expression for Passing

You've Got Mail

Gas, but I was wrong. I do not mind telling you that I have attained a higher level Of sophistication, Claire Wanzandae. Perhaps my goal of becoming a new and Worthy man is within reach after all, because no Impudent Imp such as I once Was could have ignored the hilarious name of this vessel and gone about the serious business of Diplomacy with such focus and determination. Perhaps the new Trust and Fellowship with which I am being treated by BF has caused me to rise to the occasion and act like an adult. And that is all I will say about fart-related Matters in this letter, Claire Wanzandae. On to more pressing subjects. Tallyho.

As I was saying, that feeling of nervous anticipation has been with me for the entire voyage. I wake up with it in the morning, in my hammock, and I go to sleep with it at night. Also in my hammock. It clutches at me as I stroll the deck, or laze about in a deck chair, or struggle to stay awake as B-Freezy, T-Jeff, and Johnny Adrock debate and discuss and revisit and revise and hone and tweak and dismantle and rebuild and re-debate the exact Strategy and precise Words they plan to use when we arrive in the Port of Le Havre (which is French for The Have) and make our way to the Palace of Versailles by buggy, which is going to take another Eternity—a shorter eternity than the eternity of this boat ride, but also a more tightly Packed one, since there will be four of us in the carriage and two of us are on the more Full Figured side.

You know what invention is probably the greatest one in history, Claire Wanzandae? Not the TV. Not the iPhone. Not the polio vaccine. The airplane. I never really appreciated airplanes properly before. I always thought they kind of sucked, because there you are, jammed into a tiny seat with six babies crying all around you and nothing to eat but tiny little foil packets of peanuts and pretzels, and if you ask for an extra packet the Flight Attendant gives you this Look like you just asked her to hold a Ziploc bag full of warm camel dung, although I bet they don't give you that attitude up in Business Class. But guess what? In an airplane you also arrive at your destination in a matter of Hours, wherever in the entire world you are going. It does not take a fortnight.

Also, getting on board an airplane with only one outfit is not a problem. The same cannot be said of a six-week sea voyage. Not even if you scrub your Underthings with washing powder every night. But again, I shall say no more about this unfortunate and gross hygienic Situation.

Anyway, I am all for adequate preparation, Claire Wanzandae. But there is also the risk of talking stuff to death, which is what the Founding Fathers (or the Three Windbags, as I have taken to calling them in my Head) are doing. They have planned their presentation down to the last comma, arguing about who will say what and even when those who are not currently speaking will Nod in agreement. And while I understand that a) this Audience with the King is super important, and b) there is nothing else to do on this ship but prepare and eat bad food, it still strikes me as sort of ridiculous. I mean, what if Louis XVI or his wife Marie Antoinette or for that matter some random Frenchie we don't even know about interrupts them with a question? It will throw off their whole choreography and leave them Befuddled.

I shared this concern with BF last night, as we were lying in our hammocks, listening to the sound of the boat slicing through the water beneath us, but he was Unreceptive.

"You would have us leave to Chance even one word of our audience with his Majesty?" he replied, his voice rising in Pitch. "I cannot for the life of me imagine Why."

"There is something to be said for freestyling, B-Freezy. It keeps the mind Limber."

"A limber mind is a fine thing, sonny boy. But where the future of our Republic is concerned, every *i* must be dotted, and every *t* crossed."

I was quiet for a few seconds, trying to figure out how

to say what I wanted to say next, but then the sound of slow, wheezy breathing made me realize that BF had fallen asleep, so instead of saying what I had been Planning to say, I said, "Yo! Freezinator! Wake up!"

Ben snorted and bucked around in his hammock, and made a noise like "Snuh?"

"Sorry," I said. "Were you asleep?"

Ben grunted again, as if to say "I Do Not Buy Your Didn't-Realize-You-Were-Asleep Routine."

"I think I should get to talk," I said.

"Louis XVI is not going to listen to a twelve-year-old boy."

"I'm thirteen. And Florida was my idea."

"That is immaterial."

"What if we tell him that I'm from the future?"

"Then he will think we are insane." My hammock rocked so hard I thought I was going to plummet to the ground, and then Ben was standing and his face was level with my own. "Do not be insulted," he said. "The three of us have prior relations with the king, and we have been formally enshrined as representatives of the colonies. Also, we speak French."

"Well la-di-da for you," I said, which I admit was kind of childish. "I guess I'll just take a nap in the buggy while you guys meet with the king."

"Don't be absurd," said Ben. "I'm sure you will be offered a refreshing beverage and a lovely tour of the palace."

My face burned with anger, Claire Wanzandae, but I kept my mouth shut. And from that evening on, although I am ashamed to admit it, I developed a chip on my shoulder. I kept more to myself, skipping the occasional lunch and even one dinner, and I went to bed earlier than before, instead of attending the planning sessions in T-Jeff and Johnny Adrock's room.

This did not escape notice. Jefferson asked me if I was feeling all right, and Adams took it a step further, musing at some length on the way a long journey at sea often left him "afflicted with a looseness of bowels," which was pretty much the last thing I wanted to hear over breakfast.

BF did not ask after my health, because he knew I was suffering from an affliction of the Ego, not the stomach. He gave me as much space as he could, which was not easy since my butt slept inches from his face.

* * *

Looking back on it, only a small part of my bad mood was due to getting iced out of the negotiations. Most of it was cabin fever, which is not an actual fever but a super-restless, frustrated feeling people get when they are forced to be on boats for a long time.

I know it was cabin fever because the second we stepped off the *Breakwind*, I felt better—full of energy, and also overbrimming with affection for the FFs and excitement about the mission. I was practically running circles around them, like some yippy little dog, as we walked down the gangplank and into the bustling harbor, where a number of carriages-for-hire were lined up, along with an army of merchants and laborers waiting to unload stuff from the ship, buy stuff from the ship, and rip off disoriented travelers stumbling off the ship.

I was not the only one whose Mood was one of elation as the cabin fever fell away. The Founding Fathers were full of pep too, and as soon as we stepped onto land, B-Freezy himself pointed a finger at the restaurant set a little ways back from the port, Le Seau de Cuisine ("The Bucket of Cuisine"), and said, "I propose that we celebrate the occasion of our safe arrival and fortify our appetites for the journey ahead by enjoying a sumptuous lunch at this fine seaside establishment."

Jefferson clapped a hand to his shoulder. "Even I, Benjamin Franklin of Pennsylvania's greatest antagonist in matters of State, can offer no critique of this proposal."

"I could eat a thousand *huîtres*," offered Johnny Adrock, and then elbowed me in the ribs. "That means 'oysters,' Master Ike."

"Gross," I said. I had tried an oyster once, at a Christmas party at my mom's friend Terri's house, and it was like pouring salty, cold snot down my throat.

"*Huîtres et du champagne*," said Ben, using the French word for champagne, which was *champagne*. And a few minutes later, we were sitting at Le Seau de Cuisine, with seagulls cawing overhead and a bottle of champagne in an ice bucket beside the table and the FFs going to town on a gigantic platter of raw oysters. I had a ham-and-cheese crepe, and a glass of milk.

"You are missing out," said Adams, as he slurped oyster number fourteen into his mouth. I had been counting out of boredom. Adams was in the lead, with Jefferson and B-Freezy tied at eleven.

"*You* are missing out," I retorted. "This crepe is delicious."

The final oyster tally, Claire Wanzandae, was: Johnny Adrock 16, B-Freezy 15, T-Jeff 12. By the time we piled into the carriage that was to take us to Versailles—the driver promising to switch horses every forty miles and travel through the night, so that we might arrive at the Palace in a scant twenty-five hours—it was late afternoon, all four of us were stuffed, and three of us (I think) were semi-drunk. Within minutes we had all fallen asleep.

We all woke up, famished and disoriented, sometime the following morning. Did the Founding Fathers want coffee? Croissants? No. They wanted more champagne and oysters, and they asked the driver to stop off at the nearest place where we could score some.

"Let me get this straight," I said, as the four of us tucked into an early lunch at a roadside tavern called Le Trou Dans le Mur ("The Pants Without the Ocean"). "You guys spent five and a half weeks going over every single syllable of this presentation to the king, and now here we are a few hours from Versailles, and suddenly you're all drinking champagne?"

"What are oysters without champagne?" asked T-Jeff, his mouth full of oysters and champagne.

"As a man of science," B-Freezy assured me, "let me assure you that we have ample hours to process whatever trace amounts of alcohol may enter our bloodstreams by means of this crisp, sparkling wine that pairs so beautifully with these locally harvested bivalves. Pass the bread, would you, Johnny Adrock of Massachusetts?"

"With pleasure," Adams replied.

I had another crepe. It was kind of disgusting.

"You know," I said, as they continued to gorge themselves, "we're not so near the water anymore. The seafood probably isn't as fresh."

Jefferson laughed. "If there's one thing the French know, my lad, it is how to be condescending toward people who do not speak French."

"That has not changed in two hundred and thirty-nine years," I informed him.

"But if there is a second thing the French know," he continued, "it is food." He raised his champagne flute. "Eat heartily, young Master Ike, for tomorrow we may well be on a French warship, preparing to launch a cannonball the size of John Adams's posterior at those British dogs and send them scurrying back to their master the king."

"Whatever you say, dude," I replied, clinking his flute with my glass of milk.

Ben slid another oyster down his gullet, giving him a narrow lead of twelve to eleven over Adams. "While I do enjoy our hearty colonial diet, I must say that this lighter Continental fare agrees with my digestion."

"And mine," agreed Adams.

"To the French," said Jefferson. "Our gastronomic superiors and soon-to-be saviors."

They all clinked glasses.

"Don't jinx it, you turkeys," I said.

We are about to pile back into this carriage for the last leg of the trip, so I will pick this up a little later. Hopefully to tell you that all is well and France is down to save the day. Also, I am hoping that I can slip this rather Lengthy letter into the mail once we get to Versailles, and also that there is a letter waiting for me there from you.

In any case, please keep Your fingers crossed, Claire Wanzandae. We have made it this far, but the fate of the future is still pretty much up for grabs, and I want nothing more than to Lock It Down and COME HOME.

XOXOX,
F.I.S.

CHAPTER 20

Dear Claire Wanzandae,

My hand is shaking as I write this letter. Twenty-four hours have Passed since I last put quill to parchment, and I am not exaggerating when I say that they have been the most mind-blowing and Wondrous of my life, except maybe for the twenty-four hours during which you and I first kissed.

My mind is still so scrambled and agitated that I barely know where to begin. I almost feel like the Events I am about to describe happened to someone else. Like I was outside my body, watching. Except that I was very much in my body, with all the sweat and heart-pounding thrills and terror and joy that being inside a body involves.

If I had an Eraser, I would erase all that, because it is gibberish. Let me stop trying to explain, and just explain.

Also, hopefully you have already received my Previous letter—which I was able to mail at a conveniently located French post office on the way to Versailles—so you know what I am talking about in this one, which I will begin with our Arrival at the Summer Palace of the King.

So: Our carriage was halted at the gates of Versailles by guards. I could not follow all of what was said, because it was in French, with B-Freezy doing most of the talking and the guards mostly nodding and saying "Oui, ambassadeur" a lot. And then one of them made a big sweeping gesture, and the gates swung open and the breathtaking splendor of the place nearly burned my eyeballs out of my head. I don't really feel like describing it, Claire Wanzandae, because a) I am eager to get to the important stuff, and b) I cannot do it justice. Every single type of flower you have ever seen or imagined was in bloom, except for that one that smells like rotten meat. The palace was so enormous, and so gorgeous, that it seemed impossible that it was even built for humans. Like, I couldn't imagine that anybody who got to set foot in a place like that ever had to go to the bathroom, you know what I mean? If you got to be surrounded by this type of splendor all the time, you couldn't possibly have to eat regular food to stay alive. You probably just skimmed the dew off the flowers, and maybe licked daintily at some nectar every few months. Your feet probably didn't even touch the ground.

Anyway, we rode around to the front, and a whole army of guards swarmed around us to help with our luggage, now that we had been officially Welcomed as State Guests, which was funny because all we had were two beat-up suitcases among the four of us. Some kind of Royal Welcomer—type guy ushered us into a cool, huge room with marble floors and forty-foot ceilings and oil paintings all the way up to the top of the walls, each one depicting a dead King or Queen. And then four Royal Waiter—type guys appeared and laid out a whole selection of Royal Snacks and Royal Wine for us—including me, because apparently in France as soon as you are old enough to walk, you are old enough to drink. Or else maybe because they figured I was older than I am, on account of the fact that I was kicking it with three high-ranking Personages from the Colonies. In any case, I left the wine alone.

It was a lot to take in, and luckily for me BF was translating whatever people said in French for me in a low voice, so I would have some Clue. I also caught Adams listening in, even though he claimed to speak French "like a native." From what I gathered, the King and Queen bid us the warmest of welcomes, and understood that we had come here in this manner, Unannounced and Randomly, because we were in a state of Crisis. They would see us in the Royal Gardens as soon as they had finished their afternoon session with the Royal Portrait Painter for whom they were currently Sitting.

I barely had time to cram five or six delicious Royal Pastries down my throat when some type of Royal Thing-Sayer showed up to announce that the King and Queen were ready to receive us. I stashed one more cream-filled croissant-type thing into my pocket, in case they didn't feed us again, which was a distinct possibility if they rejected our proposal for help and sent us packing, and then I scurried to catch up with B-Freezy and the others.

"Are you nervous?" I whispered as we walked down a long, dark hallway, our shoes clicking against another marble floor.

"I did not expect to be," said Ben, "as I am a seasoned diplomat. But I must confess that I do feel a peculiar rumbling in my stomach. A certain vexing discomfort, akin almost to a cramp."

"I am relieved to hear you say so," interjected Johnny Adrock. "For I, too, am experiencing a certain degree of gastronomic distress."

"As am I," added T-Jeff. "I shall, of course, ignore it."

"As will I," Johnny Adrock agreed, nodding.

"It goes without saying," said BF. "Duty first."

And then, *bam*, Claire Wanzandae. We stepped out into the dazzling Royal Gardens, which made the outer gardens look like a couple of wilted window-box daisies by comparison. It was a kaleidoscope of colors, with a long wide path in the middle, and two thrones at the end, and standing on both sides of the path were dozens of French people, advisors or noblemen or courtiers or whatever, all of them in super-formal attire, with wigs for the dudes and gigantic fancy frilly dresses for the ladies, and nobody visibly sweating even though it was a good eighty-six degrees and the sun was blazing low in the sky.

In the two thrones at the end, obviously, were the King and Queen. They looked almost like dolls from a distance, because they were so fancy and so powdered. But they started to look more real as we strolled toward them, doing that one-foot-meets-the-other walk people do when they're going down the aisle at weddings. The whole thing felt like a wedding, actually. I guess it kind of was, in the sense that we were trying to marry our Interests to theirs.

Finally, there we were, standing before King Louis XVI and Marie Antoinette. My heart was hammering against my chest, even though my official job was to Stand There and Not Say A Word. But it was at that moment, Claire, that a very weird thing happened: from the depths of my Brain, I suddenly remembered a Fact about Marie Antoinette, which was that she was going to win the Nobel Prize for discovering Radium. It was kind of amazing to think that the woman in front of me was not just the queen of France, but also a trailblazing chemist. So amazing that I decided I must be wrong. And I was correct. About being wrong, that is. The chemist was Marie Curie.

I snapped out of my Reverie of Stupidity when BF sprang into action. First, he bowed deeply to the Monarchs, which caused me, Adams, and Jefferson to quickly follow suit, as if we were a bunch of half-wits who only knew how to copy Ben, and did not feel like a particularly Great way to start.

Then Ben said, *"Bon après-midi, vos Majestés, et merci pour . . ."*

Which means, "Good afternoon, Your Majesties, and thank you for . . ."

Which is not a complete sentence, as I am sure you realize, Claire Wanzandae.

At this point, I had a strong feeling in my stomach of Yikes, because usually BF finishes his sentences, and even strings together multiple ones at once.

But as it turned out, the feeling in my stomach was not nearly as strong as the feeling in B-Freezy's stomach.

The King and Queen leaned forward and frowned, as if they were confused at the fact that their old homey Ben had suddenly stopped talking. Meanwhile, Ben got a look on his face. A look of panic.

Then Benjamin Franklin, printer, diplomat, inventor, scientist, author, etc., etc., etc., bent over and put his hands on his knees and started to vomit Profusely onto the ground.

All the courtiers or nobles or whatever gasped, and the Queen make a face like she might also puke, and turned away.

I took a step toward Ben, to see if I could help. But before I could take a second step, the situation grew rapidly Worse.

At the exact same moment, as if they were on a gold-medal-winning Olympic Synchronized Barfing team, Jefferson and Adams doubled over and began upchucking the contents of their guts, with the accompaniment of Noises that I choose not to describe here, but you can probably Imagine. Though you probably should not.

I don't know how long the three of them stood there puking, Claire Wanzandae. It might only have been a minute or two, but it felt like an Eternity. Nobody else moved, except maybe a couple of the ladies, to fan themselves with fancy fans. And the whole time, one thought kept running through my mind, over and over.

I told you guys not to eat those oysters.

But then a second thought overtook the first, and smothered it like water on a campfire. That thought was:

It's all up to you, Ike.

For a moment, I wondered why this thought sounded all garbled and weird in my brain. Then I realized that it was not a thought. It was Ben, speaking to me between fits of vomiting.

I turned to look at him.

"You can do it," he gurgled. "I believe in—"

A torrent of puke prevented him from saying the last word, but I am pretty sure it was "you." It definitely was not "oysters."

Ben's confidence filled me up with confidence of my own. Finally, he believed in me—really believed. Sure, it had taken a Puke Apocalypse for him to say so, but it still counted. I had come to save my friend and save my country, and by Jove I was going to Do it and come home if it killed me.

I cleared my throat and took a few steps forward, so as to be Heard by Louis XVI and Marie Antoinette, and also so that I might obscure their view of the disgusting things Happening behind me. All three of the Founding Fathers were lying on the ground now, still puking Intermittently and using the pauses between bouts to moan and spit and breathe heavily and mutter weak apologies in French.

"It seems I will have to speak on my friends' behalf, and my country's," I said in a loud clear voice that hopefully nobody could tell was quivering super hard.

"Who are you?" asked the king, in strongly accented but pretty solid English.

"My name is Franklin Isaac Saturday, of Philadelphia," I said. "And it is my great honor to address you this afternoon, Your Majesty. I am sorry that I do not speak French, and also that because of Bad Oysters, Mr. Franklin and Mr. Jefferson and Mr. Adams here are, um, Unwell."

"Ah," said the King, and then raised his chin and shouted at the assembled nobles or courtiers or whatever.

"Mauvaises huîtres!" he said, which I am pretty sure means "bad oysters," and everybody nodded, as if this was a totally normal thing that happened all the time. Then his gaze Returned to me. "Go on, Franklin Isaac Saturday of Philadelphia."

"Thank you, Your Majesty," I said, and then for some reason I smiled at Marie Antoinette and added "Majesties." She smiled back. Which blew my mind. But I had no time to dwell on this Development. I had to forge Ahead. I tried to remember everything the FFs had rehearsed, but all I could remember was what was supposed to have been the opening couple of lines: *We stand before you in our hour of greatest need. Our dreams of freedom something something something.*

"We stand and . . . lie here before you in our hour of greatest need," I said. "Our dreams of freedom are, uh . . . we're about to wake up from them, or—no wait, I mean, our dreams of freedom have turned into nightmares. Nightmares about an evil troll named George who wants to pull off our arms, which represent liberty from tyranny, and beat us over the head with them. But we are here today, Your Majesties, to ask you to destroy the alarm clock that is ringing in our ears, so that we can dream that impossible dream. And also we need you to step into our impossible dream, and help us vanquish the demon, I mean the troll, and, uh . . . take one small step for man, and one giant leap for mankind."

I closed my mouth. Sweat was pouring down my forehead, stinging my eyes, and I had absolutely no idea what I'd just said.

Neither, apparently, did the King and Queen. They looked at me curiously for a moment, the way you might look at a dog who has just stood up on two legs and belched the alphabet. And then in a clear, kind voice Marie Antoinette said, "Have you perhaps been struck on the head, Franklin Isaac Saturday of Philadelphia?"

I don't know how to explain what happened next, Claire Wanzandae. It was like everything went silent and dark. Not dark like black, but dark like a cloud had covered the sun. Which might be what happened, but it was like the darkness and the silence were inside me. Or I was inside them. I don't know. I might have closed my eyes. Whatever happened, I felt a sense of Calm come over me, and I thought of you, and baseball, and my little sister, Carolyn, and barbecues, and ships full of immigrants coming to Ellis Island in search of a better life, and the movie *Independence Day*, and everything that makes America great. And when reality refocused around me, I was not scared anymore. I opened my mouth and knew that another serving of Gibberish would not come out of it. Because if it did, none of those things would ever Happen.

I looked at the King, and then at the Queen. Then I turned and looked at BF, lying in a puddle of his own puke. He gave me a nod of: You Can Do It.

I gave him a nod back of: No Duh, Sherlock.

And then, Claire Wanzandae, I started all over again.

"Forgive me, Your Majesties. And please forget my nervous words. So much depends on this Audience, and though I am no diplomat, no statesman, no politician, but merely a humble child, I shall try to convey to you our most urgent request."

Louis XVI turned to Marie Antoinette and said, in English, "You fixed him!" Everybody laughed, including me.

I turned and gestured at the fallen Fathers. "The America for which these men and many others have worked so hard is about to be crushed before it breathes its first free breath," I said. "Only the great nation of France can save us from the wrath of King George."

"I hate that guy," said Louis XVI, his face reddening beneath the powder.

"Oui," said Marie Antoinette. "Such a stick-in-the-mud. Always praying. No sense of style at all."

"Totally," I said. "And now's your chance to show him who's boss. Send us some troops, and some money, and we'll humiliate him so bad he'll never recover. The British Empire will be a laughingstock. And France will be the undisputed heavyweight champion of the world."

I nearly smacked myself in the forehead when I heard that phrase, which I must have gotten from Saturday morning wrestling, jump out of my mouth. But Louis XVI smiled, and rubbed his hands together. They were surprisingly small.

"The undisputed heavyweight champion of the world,"

he repeated in his French accent. "I like this expression. But risking the lives of my army and navy, which are the finest in the world, this I do not so much like. There is, after all, more to life than defeating the British. There is also defeating the Spanish. And defeating the Dutch. *Sacre bleu*, do I hate the Dutch!"

"We'll make it worth your while," I said quickly, before he could get distracted. "America and France can be great friends, Your Majesty. In time, we will be a very powerful country, and we will never forget our debts."

"A powerful country, he says." Marie Antoinette laughed. "How adorable, that he thinks so."

My first impulse was to tell her a few choice facts about how big and rich and important America was going to be, but then it occurred to me that maybe it was better if they didn't know all that, in case they started getting ideas of their own about taking the place over, and I changed my tune.

"Or not," I said. "I mean, who knows, right? Obviously we'll never be the center of the world, like France is. Frankly, I'd be happy if we even achieved one tenth of the, um, sophistication and mightiness and downright class of—"

"What is it you offer me?" interrupted Louis XVI, who had somehow obtained a chicken leg, and was chewing on it as he spoke. "Or do you believe that America's friendship and the privilege of defeating the British will sway me to your cause?"

I opened my mouth to answer, then waited until a particularly loud and gross Salvo from Thomas Jefferson was finished.

"Again," I said, "sorry about them. I knew that seafood place was too far from the ocean."

"Tell me its name," said the King, "and I will have the proprietor beheaded. This is foul in the utmost."

"Truly, it is a sickening and horrible display," said Marie Antoinette. "Perhaps they ought to eat some bread? To calm their stomachs?"

Louis XVI snapped his fingers. *"Pain!"* he shouted, and two Royal Attendant-type people scurried off to find a pan. Or so I thought. They came back a second later with three loaves of French bread, which is how I learned that *pain*, which sounds like pan, is French for bread. Though pans would have been more helpful, since at least the Founding Fathers could have thrown up into those. Whereas aside from nodding weakly, there wasn't much they would do with the bread. Still, it was the thought that counted.

Marie Antoinette watched, disappointed that they weren't eating the bread. "How about some cake?" she suggested, but I could tell her heart wasn't in it.

"My Queen is kind," said Louis XVI, by way of dismissing her suggestion. "But we were discussing matters of state, were we not?"

"We were, Your Majesty. And no, of course I do not expect you to help us out of friendship alone. I'm about to make you an offer you can't refuse. Are you ready?"

"I am ready."

"How about you, Your Majesty?" I asked Marie Antoinette. "Are you ready?"

"I am ready."

I waited a moment, getting into the spirit of showbiz, then shook my head the way Igbert Fibbelstream used to and said, "Nah, I don't think you're ready. I need you to be *really* ready."

"Delay a moment further and I shall have you flogged!" thundered Louis XVI, who was turning out to be kind of unpredictable and also a jerk.

"Okay," I said. "Sorry. Our offer is . . ."

They leaned forward in their thrones. I waited a tiny fraction of a second, and then threw my hands in the air like some kind of deranged game show host and said, "Florida!"

"Florida," mused Louis XVI, stroking his chin.

"The richest and largest part of our Continent," I said. "A

massive, fertile land of timber and sugar, gold and silver."
That last part was probably not true, but then again, maybe
it was. I didn't know much about Florida, really. Timber just
meant trees, so that seemed reasonable, at least.

"A British colony," he said.

"Not for long. King George is sending all his troops north,
to fight us in Massachusetts and Pennsylvania and, uh, you
know, Delaware. The second your troops help us defeat the
redcoats, they can jump in some ships, cruise down to Florida,
and stick a French flag in it." My mind was racing. It actually
made sense, this stuff I was saying. "And it's surrounded
by water," I said. "No borders to worry about, except with
your good buddy America. And did I mention that whoever
controls Florida controls the citrus trade? The oranges are just
dropping off the trees down there. Grapefruits, too." Florida
was starting to sound so good, I almost forgot how much I
hated it. "Plus, from there you can bully Britain out of the
whole Caribbean! They'll fold like a house of cards!"

Louis XVI gestured at me with a pastry. Apparently,
this was a working lunch for him. "Much of what you say
is intriguing, Franklin Isaac Saturday. The rest is nonsense,
but . . ."

He trailed off. I waited, resisting the urge to ask him which part was nonsense and also becoming suddenly, acutely aware of how badly I had to pee.

The silence was compromised by some loud retching from BF and Johnny Adrock. I could tell who was who without looking now. They each had their own unique puking styles.

Marie Antoinette turned to her husband and raised her eyebrows. "I do like grapefruit," she said.

Louis XVI patted her hand. "And I hate England," he said. "King George is the kind of man who looks like he carries a dead mackerel around in his trousers."

I had no idea what that meant, but it certainly sounded insulting. Maybe it was a poor translation from French or something. In any case, it didn't seem to matter.

"He sure does," I agreed. "Maybe even two mackerels. So do we have a deal?"

Louis XVI picked up a wine goblet and took a long, slurpy sip. I looked around, and wondered if all these nobles or courtiers or whatever just gathered in their finery every day to watch him gorge himself. And what about Marie Antoinette? Why wasn't she eating? Was it just because there were a bunch of dudes throwing up in front of her, or was Louis XVI so rude that he ate before she did, or what?

"I need more," he said, and grinned what a more Uncouth man than Yours Truly might call a poop-eating grin. "What else have you to offer me, Franklin Isaac Saturday of Philadelphia?"

"The exclusive right to sell wine in America," I said, pulling it right out of my butt. I glanced behind me at Ben, and he gave me a weak nod of approval. Or disapproval. It was hard to tell, and also too late, since I had already Said it.

"Interesting," the King murmured.

"Worth a fortune," I replied. "We are a people who have real problems with alcohol."

"People do not realize that we French also distill the world's finest spirits," he said, a little petulantly. "We are renowned for our wine, and rightly so. But French brandy is delicious beyond compare. French rum rivals any in the world, though we are not a sugar-producing country."

"You are now," I pointed out. "Thanks to Florida."

That earned me a grin.

He drained his wine, and said, "The exclusive right to sell both wine and spirits in America. And also cheese. Have you tasted our French cheese? I am doing you a favor."

"As you wish, Your Majesty," I said. "I love cheese." And I bowed.

King Louis XVI cackled and lifted his wine goblet, which had been refilled the instant it was empty. "Then let us destroy King George!" he bellowed, and the whole place started cheering.

CHAPTER 21

From the Journal of Benjamin Franklin

I trust that by this juncture I, Benjamin Franklin, have made it abundantly apparent that I am an efficient man. That all I have accomplished in the fourscore minus ten years I have been a resident of this planet could not have reached fruition had I not the ability to perform acts with a high degree of simultaneity. To wit, while flying a kite to prove that electricity existed in storm clouds in the form of lightning, I was concurrently devising a rod that would attract lightning in order to protect structures from that insidious force of destruction. And at the same time I was inventing the lending library,

I made note that the world would soon require the introduction of a long extending arm to retrieve books from upper shelves. And, for reasons mysterious even to myself, it was while whispering sweet words of affection to my beloved wife, Deborah, that I came up with the idea for swim fins.

I deem it necessary to cite this so it will not come as a surprise when I say that during the throes of my violent gastrointestinal upheaval, I made a mental note to lavish enormous praise on Ike for the way he comported himself before King Louis XVI and Marie Antoinette if and when the Tossed Oysters Festival came to a conclusion. When I said I believed in him and that he could do it, I had intended to inspire, but I also believed in my own word. Prior judgments to the contrary notwithstanding, he is as capable and quick a lad as ever I have encountered, and indeed he gives me Hope that the future is not so utterly debased as I had previously Thought. Not only was his speech the quintessential display of diplomacy performed under the most regrettable circumstances, it may very well have righted the course of our collective mission to gain independence from the Mother country.

As well as the course of my own legacy.

I must also confess that whilst experiencing that bout of reverse peristalsis, it crossed my mind that Ike's legacy might nullify my own. Had I not already been voiding the contents of my stomach, this thought might have caused me to Do so.

As I have Admitted before, and with chagrin, my public persona is of paramount concern to me. Perhaps too much so, as my own self-regard can lead to folly, as was the case in my feud with Ike during the Medicine Show episode, when I should have apologized and did Not. Of course, my passion for our future nation is greater than my need for personal recognition, but at the same time I am not taciturn about the contributions I have rendered for that cause. I take immeasurable pride in what I have done, and I bask in the admiration that was, until so recently, afforded me by my fellow colonists. I thrilled to hear such statements as these as I perambulated the streets of Philadelphia:

"Thanks for all you've done for our cause, Mr. Franklin!"

"It's an honor to be heated by a Franklin stove, Mr. Franklin!"

"I enjoy urinating through your urinary catheter, Mr. Franklin!"

From what Ike has told me of the future, I am to continue being admired by citizens of the United States of America for generations to come. Public buildings shall bear my name. Universities. Bridges. Stamps.

But here is the quandary that has kept me awake these past few nights: Will all that remain true if the French army is unsuccessful in its efforts to secure our Independence, or will my good name be reduced to a mere footnote appended to a failed effort? Or even worse, am I to become an object of historical vilification by dint of the belief that I and the other members of the Committee of Five purposely undermined the dream of Independence?

Even if the colonists and the French succeed, shall I be remembered as one whose actions nearly prevented Liberty from being achieved?

My relationships with Messrs. Thomas Jefferson

of Virginia, John Adams of Massachusetts, Robert Livingston of New York, and Robert Sherman of Connecticut have, at times, been combative. Clashing self-images and petty wanting have been very much at the core of that strife. However, I *can* say without any fear of contradiction that the intention of all involved was to advance the greater good of our fellow colonists. The thought that our once-good names will be forever sullied gives me greater discomfort than any number of bad oysters.

Such are my thoughts as I sit in a café on the Parisian street known as the Rue de Jacques Bernoulli, awaiting Ike's emergence from the *toilette*. He and I have chosen to take leave of Messrs. Jefferson and Adams, who are spending this balmy afternoon salmon fishing in the Seine, and partake of a delicious lunch.

I have grown very fond of Ike. And not only because he venerates me in a way that I once took for granted and have now been otherwise denied. Perhaps one day in the future he will be recognized for his role in our democracy. That is unobjectionable to me. As long as I, too, am deemed a hero by posterity. This possibility now seems more and more remote, both in the darkness of night and in the brightness of the Parisian day.

"I'm back from the sale de bains," Ike announced unnecessarily, mispronouncing the French word for *bathroom* as he retook his seat at our table by the window. I prefer restaurant tables by the window, especially in Paris where I can appreciate the beauty of the women as they saunter along, and they in turn can have their beauty affirmed by me, a world-renowned connoisseur of feminine charm.

"I could eat a hundred of these croissants," he said, grabbing what was by my count his third of the meal and sixth of the day, which might have explained his frequent, lengthy trips to the sale de bains.

"It's pronounced cwa-sant," I corrected him. "C-r-o-i-s-s-a-n-t. Cwa-sant."

"Where's the *w*?"

"There is no *w*."

"So what's with the cwa?"

"It's French. They pronounce the *r* as a *w*."

"Then why isn't the name of their country pronounced Fwance?"

I would be dishonest if I said that did not give

me pause, but I ignored the question and pursued the conversation that was the point of this lunch.

"So," I began, "Today we shall be expected at the harbor to attend the departure of the Marquis de Lafayette—"

"The who de what?"

"The nineteen-year-old general who has been dispatched to aid the colonists in their cause. He is leaving today. And though this may be difficult for you to hear, I do not think we should accompany him on that first ship, to a place still in turmoil, a place that regards us as persona non grata."

"No, B-Freezy—" he began. But I was not of a mind to hear out his objections, as this was a matter I had contemplated endlessly during those long, sleepless nights spent tossing hither and yon on the finest of French featherbeds.

"Understand, Ike. I know you want to provide further assistance to the colonists, but as objects of scorn and derision, we would be a distraction from their most important task at hand, which is to rally behind Generals Washington and Lafayette to defeat the Tory army and achieve our independence. I submit that instead, we wait some weeks and take the next ship, so that with any luck by the time we reach the colonies they will be winning handily and we will be lauded for our efforts. Rather than potentially be pursued by angry mobs for them, as I have been before."

Ike remained silent, his face contorted to the point where it was difficult for me to ascertain whether he was merely pensive, or angry at me for thwarting his plans.

Finally, he looked at me with full, watery eyes, and I realized I had misunderstood the emotion delaying his response.

"That's not what I want at all."

"I know, Ike, but we are now at war, and it would be foolhardy to—"

"No," he interrupted. "You don't get it, B-Freezy. There's only one place I want to go, and it's home. My home."

He reached into his pocket, and removed a folded envelope.

"This came today," he said quietly, and withdrew a page covered in the unmistakably charming handwriting of Claire Wanzandae.

CHAPTER 22

Dear Ike,

I hope one way or another this letter reaches you. I sent one copy to BF's mailbox in Philadelphia and another to Versailles. Maybe you are in neither of those places. Maybe you are on a French warship, and you will not receive this letter for several weeks. That would be really bad, though. I will explain why in a minute. First, I want to tell you how proud I am. Because you did it, Ike. You saved America. You said you were going to, and you did. I knew you could, though I will admit I had no idea How. But there was something about the look on your face when you climbed into that box, something serious and steady and very, very handsome about your eyes that I could see even through the airholes in the cardboard when I said good-bye. I thought to myself, We are all in Ike's hands now. And whenever I got nervous, either because you didn't write or because you did and instead of fixing the future you were busy surviving as Igbert Fibbelstream, I thought back to that moment and that look in your eyes, and used that to calm myself.

I am not going to lie to you, Ike. The news I have for you is not good news. Do not freak out. Nobody is dead and nothing is unfixable, but it needs to be fixed right now, and the fixer is you. I know you probably feel like you need to see the war through, and make sure everything turns out right, but you do not have time to do that. You are needed here.

So this is it, Ike: Your mom is in the hospital. Her arm is broken, and so is her nose, and she has a minor concussion. Like I said, it could be worse. A couple of broken bones are not that big a deal, and actually the nose is made of cartilage, not bone, so when we say it is broken, technically speaking, we are wrong. But let me explain why these things are broken and concussed, and maybe you will understand.

They are broken and concussed because she got in a car accident two days ago, right after dropping your little sister off at school. Somebody rear-ended her, and her air bag went off and caused these injuries, which is a thing that happens sometimes. But why did someone rear-end her? Because she fell asleep behind the wheel, and her foot came down on the brake for no reason, causing the car to suddenly screech to a stop in the middle of the block and get smashed from behind. And why did she fall asleep at the wheel? Because she is not sleeping at night. Like, not a wink.

And why is she not sleeping a wink? I think you know, Ike. There is only so much reassurance a mother can take from letters. She wants her son back, even if he claims to be safe and a yoga prodigy referred to as The One by all the counselors at his top secret yoga retreat. Which, incidentally, was laying it on kind of thick. I know I told you to make her feel safe, but I cannot help but wonder if that was really the most calming and convincing story you could come up with. I know you had to write it really fast, before the *Breakwind* left the harbor, but come on, dude. Most extremely calming and convincing stories do not have ninjas in them.

Anyway, back to your mother. For a while she was taking sleeping pills, but then she got scared that she would become addicted to them, so she stopped. And also stopped sleeping. Instead she just lies in bed, staring at the ceiling and wondering where you are and when you are coming back and pondering what she did wrong and how maybe she should have sent you to a counselor when she and your dad split up and thinking about your relationship with Dirk and asking herself if she has been selfish and thought of herself when she should have been thinking of her son.

I know all this because I have been going to visit her in the hospital every day after school, and we sit and talk. Mostly, I listen. She is very open. In a weird way, we have become friends. Except that she does not fully trust me, because she suspects that I know where you are and will not tell her. Which is obviously true, and makes me feel about twenty-seven different kinds of horrible, and the only reason I have not told her the truth, Ike, is that it would worry her even more. Or she would not believe it, and our friendship would be ruined.

So basically, it is time for you to come back here. Your country needed you, and so did your friend. And because you are a good person, a heroic person, you went where you were needed.

Now your family needs you. And what does it matter, you saving America, if you come home and the people you left behind have been destroyed? Not by a new history creeping over the old, but by your own absence?

You get it. I will not say any more. I will just check my doorstep for a giant Colonial or French box with breathing holes cut in it, which I know in my heart of hearts will be arriving very soon.

Speaking of history, and space-time, and all that stuff: Nothing has rippled forward yet, and I have a new theory about why. Because according to my old theory about points of no return and historic milestones and all that, things already should have changed. But Florida is still a national embarrassment, non-French wine and spirits are still available for purchase, and there is nothing on Wikipedia or in the books at the library about BF and T-Jeff and Johnny Adrock going to France in 1776. Nor is there any mention of a historic speech by Franklin Isaac Saturday.

So here is my new theory. Are you ready?

My new theory is that nothing will change until you travel back to 2015. That you are in a kind of bubble universe right now, and the events you have caused are locked off from the flow of time outside it until you pierce the bubble and the contents start to ooze out, and ooze forward.

I am no theoretical physicist, and I would be the first to admit that I do not have any idea what I am talking about, but sometimes a girl has to try to understand time travel even if she is flying blind. If I am right, though, then everything we undid with the map and the Claireike, and also everything you redid by mailing yourself back, will take effect and become the New History the moment you return here. Quite frankly, this is terrifying. I mean, who knows what No Florida, or rather French Florida, will mean to the history of this country? For that matter, who knows how the total lack of a domestic cheese industry might affect farming, and cuisine, and countless lives? Maybe a French monopoly on wine and spirits means we never had Prohibition? Or maybe Prohibition caused a war with France? Maybe JFK was never president, since his dad made his fortune smuggling booze into the country? Maybe I am still never born, due to some cheese-, Florida-, or booze-related event in my family's distant past that has now been erased? I will not pretend I am not scared, Ike. A person could go crazy thinking about this stuff, especially with no one to talk to about it.

But I am also at peace, and ready to accept whatever happens, because I am certain you did your best. And who knows? Maybe the world is an infinitely better place because of what you did. Maybe you will puncture the bubble and return to find that we have world peace, or better Star Wars prequels.

And maybe you will also return to a Claire Wanzandae who has never met you. Or a mother who never had children. Or was never born herself. I do not know what happens then, Ike. I cannot think about it without sweating and feeling like I want to puke. So I am making a choice, and that choice is to have faith that everything will turn out fine and dandy.

There is only one way to find out.

I am waiting for you, Ike. Please do not make me wait too long.

I would rather risk everything than lose you to the past.

I am still and hopefully will remain,
Your Girlfriend, Claire Wanzandae

CHAPTER 23

When you've gotta go, you've gotta go.

More specifically, when your Absence is tearing apart the lives of the people you left behind, and anyway you are too puny and too poorly versed in the art of sticking a British soldier in the gut with a bayonet to make a major difference in the War for Independence, and also you are stuck across the ocean from that war, and also you have saved America's bacon once already, you've gotta go.

I read Claire's letter, which had been hand-delivered to me by some kind of Royal Hand-Deliverer right before I went to lunch with BF, and I knew it in my heart and stomach and also my Brain. And since that is the main Triumvirate of organs on which I rely for guidance, it was an easy decision. Not easy like "Sure, I'll Have Fries With That," but easy like "What choice do I have?"

I'm not going to lie. It also occurred to me that if Claire's new theory was right, then a) I might bust out of this bubble universe only to find everything and everyone I loved different or nonexistent or all of humankind enslaved to a race of giant ants, though that last part was probably unlikely, and b) by the same logic, if I stayed put then the bubble universe would stay a bubble, and history would remain unchanged by all the shenanigans and mishaps and quick-witted and slow-witted Stuff I had done without properly understanding the ramifications of my Actions any more than a bird understands what's going to happen when it flies into the engine of a 747.

Also, c) I had a really nice daydream about Claire Wanzandae growing up to be a Theoretical Physicist, and coming home after a long day at her Lab and taking off her white coat and meanwhile I've made her a delicious and complicated dinner involving Duck and lit romantic candles, and she gives me a big smile and all the pressures of her high-stress job just fall away, and she hangs up the lab coat on top of her Nobel Prize statue and I pull out her chair for her even though we are married and eat dinner together all the time, because it's just the type of chivalrous individual I am.

So for a split second, I hesitated. I wondered whether it was nobler to sacrifice myself to the past, so that a) would never happen.

But then I thought about my mother. And also about c). That was when I ding-dinged the little silver bell Marie Antoinette had given me, which immediately caused a Royal Bell-Answerer to come running. My French was still not very good, since my strategy of learning the language by eating upward of fifteen croissants a day had been mostly a failure. To communicate with these guys I usually went through BF or one of the other Founding Fathers. But right now BF was in the bathroom, and also I didn't want him to hear what I was going to say, in case he tried to stop me.

"*Oui?*" said the Royal Bell-Answerer. "*De quoi avez-vous besoin?*"

That meant "What do you need?" It was what they said every time.

"*Un* . . . box," I said, since I didn't know the word for box. I made the outline of a box with my hands, then said, "*Enorme.*"

The Royal Bell-Answerer stared at me blankly, and yet also with contempt. It was a look these guys had down pat, believe me.

"A box," I repeated, louder this time, because for some reason when people didn't speak English I tended to assume they would understand it better if I shouted.

"Big enough for me to sit in!" I shouted. The Royal Bell-Answerer looked at me as if he had suddenly found something unexpected and strange-tasting in his mouth.

"Je ne comprends pas," he said.

"Then find somebody who does!" I bellowed, feeling myself slip into an Unreasonable state. I guess because the decision I had made was so momentous that I felt like I had to make it happen right now, before I lost my nerve.

"Obtenir le tronc spécial que j'avais conçu," I heard, and turned to see BF waddling toward me, with a grave look on his face and a large pastry in his hand.

The Royal Bell-Answerer nodded and turned on his heel and speed-walked off. Ben strode up to me, put a hand on my shoulder, and sighed.

"I suppose this is good-bye, sonny boy."

"Not if you come with me," I said without thinking. "Tell him to get a box big enough for us both."

As soon as I said it, I had a feeling of Uh-Oh, What Did I Just Do? And suddenly, I understood what BF had probably felt when I sent him that letter offering to come visit the past: an overwhelming desire for it not to happen, despite all the love and Family Feelings that had developed between the two of us over the last few weeks. Because if he came with me, BF would be two hundred and thirty-nine years Behind, and also one hundred percent my responsibility. I would have to get him up to speed and make sure he didn't make a fool of himself, plus people might recognize him from the hundred-dollar bill, if he was still on it, and be like Yo, What's Up With That Dude?

On the other hand, I probably needed all the help I could get, and there are worse things than having a world-class genius by your side, even if he is a little bit outdated. Plus, it was no less than what he had done for me. And on the third hand, if giant ants did rule the planet, at least I would have somebody Plump and Delicious with me to distract them while I made a break for the secret underground caves where the Resistance lived.

But before I could work myself up into a state of Freaking Out over all these possibilities, BF shook his head and smiled.

"Thank you, Ike. But no. Just as you have your place, so do I. And it is here."

I could feel myself starting to tear up a little bit. I didn't want Ben to come with me, but I also wasn't ready to say good-bye. So instead I just nodded.

"I pray that the future is all it once was. Or perhaps even more."

"Yeah," I said, my heart starting to beat really fast. "Me too."

"This is not good-bye," said Ben, putting a hand on my shoulder. "We shall remain friends no matter what. I expect a full report, as soon as you are able to write. And perhaps a visit, when things have calmed down in our respective Worlds."

"I don't know if I've got the stomach to come back here again," I said. "It takes a lot out of a guy, this time travel stuff."

"I meant that I would visit you," Ben said. "You moron." But he said it with a wink, the way a grandfather would.

"I guess that'd be okay," I said slowly. "Assuming everything is, you know, okay back there."

"Things have a way of turning out fine," Ben said, in a voice that was obviously meant to sound all-knowing and reassuring—and actually kind of succeeded, even though we both knew he had no idea what he was talking about.

"I should very much like to someday learn of my standing

in the eyes of future generations," he said dreamily, with a far-off look in his eyes.

"Let me get this straight. What you're most curious about in the future is not new inventions or ideas or innovations, but what people think about you?"

Ben's cheeks turned pinkish for a moment, then returned to their normal color. "Well, of course, those as well," he said. "Naturally, as a man of science."

"Uh-huh."

He drew himself up to his full height, and bowed slightly to me. That was when I noticed that the Royal Bell-Answerer was back, and he was hauling some kind of steamer-trunk-type thing behind him. It was plastered with postage stamps and pocked with breathing holes, and the inside was covered in what looked like purple velvet.

"I had this designed specially," said BF. "Franklin Isaac Saturday, I wish you safe travels."

He extended his hand.

I ignored it, and gave him a hug. After a moment, he returned it.

"Promise you'll write," he said, and then we both started crying.

CHAPTER 24

Dear Ben,

Dude. I don't even know where to start.

I guess with an apology for not writing sooner. I know it has been more than a month since my Return Journey, which means that you might be in any number of places: back in Philly, or aboard a French warship heading across the Atlantic, or maybe still at Versailles, stuffing your face with pastry. I guess you didn't know where you'd be either, which is why you cleverly Stashed a crazy amount of both French and Colonial postage into the specially designed travel-coffin or whatever that you had made for me. That was pretty slick, and so was filling it up with croissants and cool, refreshing lemonade. That's why you're my main man, B-Freezy.

You've Got Mail

I meant to write sooner, but it has been a full-time job getting re-acclimated to the world—which is Notably different than I left it, though that is the understatement of the year and really more like the understatement of the last two hundred and thirty-nine years.

I will start with the Big Picture stuff, since I know you must be curious about that. Let me begin by saying: Your legacy has held up reasonably well. History does not remember you as some bumbling bozo who spilled jelly on the Declapendence. You are still on the hundred-dollar bill, although it is worth somewhat less than it used to be due to the Smaller size of the country, which I will get to in a minute. Your name still Adorns all kinds of stuff here in Philly, from elementary schools to cheesesteak restaurants, not that you had anything to do with the invention of the cheesesteak unless you have been holding Out on me. You are still remembered as a Founding Father, diplomat, inventor, printer, scientist, etc., etc., etc., although if you want total honesty then yes, the Oyster Incident is also remembered in the history books and a slang term for throwing up in a high-stakes situation is "pulling a Franklin." I can hear you fuming all the way from here about how unfair that is, so let me assure you that "pulling an Adams" and "pulling a Jefferson" are also terms for Inopportune Barfing.

You will also be happy to know that the United States of America has endured. Our victory in the War of Independence was swift and decisive, with a combination of French and Colonial troops overwhelming the British forces in a couple of early battles and King George basically throwing in the towel. In fact, B-Freezy, the war was a lot less bloody and deadly than the old version, so in that sense my entire mission of Boneheaded Helping was actually a success.

In other ways, However, the consequences are less straightforwardly swell, and more Extremely Weird, although of course I am the only person alive who thinks so (besides Claire Wanzandae, who I will get to in a minute, but rest assured that CLAIRE IS STILL CLAIRE! and CLAIRE IS STILL MY GIRLFRIEND!), because for everybody else, the way things are is just the way they've always been.

In any case, the deal I made with King Louis XVI is still in effect, and the French still own Florida. They also continue to hold a monopoly on the sale of wine and spirits in America. As far as I can tell, both these things have worked out okay. Florida is way cooler under French rule than it ever was under ours, for one thing. Instead of a festering alligator-infested swamp full of sun-addled trash-eating lunatics, it's a swanky vacation destination with great food and this European vibe that has kind of rubbed off and made the rest of our country a whole lot classier. The French have even figured out some amazing ways to cook alligator.

The wine-and-spirits thing has also been basically a win, because instead of a nation of beer-swilling doofuses sitting on our couches eating snacks made of reconstituted potato granules, we are now a nation with refined tastes, and we tend to walk more and be less fat and lazy. We even watch less TV, which means nothing to you of course and I don't feel like explaining it now, but basically we spend less time staring at a box that turns us into total morons.

A lot of History is also somewhat different due to the French control of the booze industry—for example, from what I have read we almost went to war with France when we tried to pass a law outlawing booze in the early part of the twentieth century. And because we never passed that law, Prohibition never existed, which means that some of my favorite old-time gangster movies either never got made or are totally different. And also, possibly unrelated or possibly not, Frank Sinatra never became a star because he was never born. There are probably a ton of other examples of this kind of thing, but since I have only been here a month, I don't have the full lay of the land yet. I'm picking up on more stuff every day as I

BENJAMiN FRANKLIN

read and speak to people, though. To give another example, yesterday I made a reference to the Yankees being the greatest dynasty in the history of baseball, and Ryan Demphill looked at me like I was crazy and said, "Yeah right, dude. The Yankees have never even made the World Series." I haven't had time to figure out why that is. Does it have something to do with French Florida? With booze? With somebody who no longer dies in the Revolutionary War? Is it a series of tiny little things that I'd never be able to untangle no matter how long I tried? I realize you have no idea what I'm talking about, because baseball hasn't been invented yet, but Whatever.

Mainly, I have been very Lucky, because my family was not directly affected by my time traveling shenanigans. I still live with my mom and Caro and Dirk the Jerk, who is still a jerk, though he drinks Brandy instead of beer. My dad lives in Florida, not California, because that is where the French film industry is based, so I get to see him more often and he speaks French and wears more striped shirts than he used to and is much happier than I remember him being, probably because he's remarried to a French woman named Lana who is cool and pregnant with my future half brother or sister. So again: a win for Young Master Ike.

Except that Franklin Isaac Saturday is no longer my name.

This time around, I am named after a different great hero of the Early Days of American Democracy: the general who led the war effort against the British.

In other words, B-Freezy, I am now Lafayette Marcel Saturday. And this is not a weird name at all. There are three other Lafayettes at my junior high.

Oh yeah. My junior high. Guess what it is called?

Franklin Isaac Saturday Junior High.

It's one the most popular school names in the country, BF. You know why? Because Franklin Isaac Saturday is the single biggest, most famous hero of the Revolution—an inspiration to children across the nation and proof that kids can make a difference. His Oration at Versailles is memorized by every sixth grader in America, and dramatic performance competitions are held every year on—you guessed it—Franklin Isaac Saturday Day.

He is especially famous because a) he disappeared so mysteriously right after his famous speech, and b) no one knows what he looked like or where he came from. Which, again, is a giant stroke of luck for me, since *Oh my gosh you're a dead ringer for the most beloved kid in American history and you also have the same last name!* would get old very fast.

So there it is, B-Freezy. For a man like you who places such importance on legacy, maybe it would be super-frustrating for nobody to know what you had Done. But I don't feel that way at all. For me, just knowing is enough. Better, even. I like having a secret.

And I *really* like sharing that secret with Claire Wanzandae.

You see, Ben, she also remembers the past—the old past. History rewrote itself for everybody else, but because we were exchanging letters the whole time she had a toe in the pool, so to speak, and she remembers the way things used to be. At least, we think that's why. She knows who I really am, and what I did. And when we are alone, taking a walk in the park or sitting in a corner of the school cafeteria sharing a delicious peanut butter and jelly Claireike (as they are now known) she calls me by my old name.

So there it is, BF. You were right. Everything has turned out pretty well, though of course there are times when I feel Unsettled and Confused, and even Isolated from everybody else because I lived through such momentous events and have experienced things in both the distant Colonial past and the alternate future that they never can and never will. But for the most part, life is pretty sweet. You should come visit sometime. I miss you, and I would Welcome the chance to show you around. Plus, Claire Wanzandae is dying to meet you.

I am including Ample postage in this letter in hopes that you will take me up on this invitation Soon. And until we meet again, Ben Franklin, I will be on the lookout for Delivery of a large box containing a Founding Father, statesman, inventor, printer, author, politician, scientist, musician, philosopher, creator of the postal system, and good, good Friend.

With love,
Lafayette Marcel (Franklin Isaac) Saturday

Tyler Lipman

An original *Saturday Night Live* writer, **ALAN ZWEIBEL** has won multiple Emmy and Writers Guild of America Awards for his work in television, which also includes *It's Garry Shandling's Show, Late Show with David Letterman*, and *Curb Your Enthusiasm*. In the theater he collaborated with Billy Crystal on the Tony Award–winning play *700 Sundays* and wrote the off-Broadway play *Bunny Bunny: Gilda Radner: A Sort of Romantic Comedy*, which he adapted from his book, and his novel *The Other Shulman* won the 2006 Thurber Prize for American Humor.

Matthew L. Kaplan

ADAM MANSBACH is the author of the instant *New York Times* best sellers *Go the **** to Sleep* and *You Have to ******* Eat*, as well as the novels *Rage Is Back, The Dead Run, Angry Black White Boy*, and *The End of the Jews*, winner of the California Book Award. His work has appeared in the *New Yorker*, the *New York Times Book Review, Esquire*, the *Believer*, and on National Public Radio's *All Things Considered, The Moth*, and *This American Life*. He also wrote the screenplay for the 2016 motion picture *Barry*.

Together, Adam and Alan are the authors of the first book in this series, *Benjamin Franklin: Huge Pain in My . . .*